DINOTOPIA
THE EXPLORERS

A WORD FROM DINOTOPIA® CREATOR
JAMES GURNEY

Dinotopia began as a series of large oil paintings of lost cities. One showed a city built in the heart of a waterfall. Another depicted a parade of people and dinosaurs in a Roman-style street. It occurred to me that all these cities could exist on one island. So I sketched a map, came up with a name, and began to develop the story of a father and son shipwrecked on the shores of that island. *Dinotopia,* which I wrote and illustrated, was published in 1992.

The surprise for me was how many readers embraced the vision of a land where humans lived peacefully alongside intelligent dinosaurs. Many of those readers spontaneously wrote music, performed dances, and even made tree house models out of gingerbread.

A sandbox is much more fun if you share it with others. With that in mind, I invited a few highly respected authors to join me in exploring Dinotopia. The mandate for them was to embellish the known parts of the world before heading off on their own to discover new characters and new places. Working closely with them has been a great inspiration to me. I hope you, too, will enjoy the journey.

James Gurney

Windy Point

Crystal Caverns

The Hatchery

Baz

Pooktook

Volcaneum

Hudro
Swamp

Waterfall City

Sculpted Cliffs

Cornucopia
Treetown
Bent Root

Palongo River

Temple Ruins

NORTHERN PLAINS

CRACKSHELL POINT

BACKBONE MOUNTAINS

Rocky Pass

Prosperine

Sapphire Bay

Poseidos
(sunken)

RAINY
BASIN

GREAT CANAL

SKY GALLEY CAVES

Deep Lake

Warmwater
Bay

Culebra

OUTER ISLAND

Amu River

Tentpole of the Sky

Thermala

The Time Towers

Sky City

Canyon City

Ancient Gorge

Red Rapid
Canyon

The Portal

The Sentinels

GREAT DESERT

FORBIDDEN MOUNTAINS

Pteros

Sauropolis

Dolphin Bay

Dragonfly Coast

Chandara

BLACKWOOD
FLATS

Cape Turtletail

PROLOGUE

Like a wretched, stinking dragon, the fire exhaled billowing clouds of dark, acrid smoke. From her classroom window, fourteen-year-old Lian watched as the crackling flames ignited nearby trees.

As the courageous villagers tried to beat it back, Lian was forced to gather up her frightened students and lead them up a winding trail to the safety of the high caves.

Lian fought the urge to glance back. If she did, her students might, too. And it was not a sight she wished them to see.

"Eyes on the trail. Look ahead!" she urged her young charges.

Soon they approached the yawning mouth of a cave, where jade and amber lanterns hung to dispel the darkness. Figures waited near the cave's entrance, a pair of young Mussaurus.

The plant-eating dinosaurs walked on all fours and had large round heads with big eyes and short necks. They were small, only five feet from the tips of their snouts to the ends of their tails. Their scales were a soft purple, like a grape's skin, and the lantern light cast yellow and green highlights on their proud flanks and thick tails.

Each dinosaur wore sparkling crystal necklaces and rings, and small carts filled with supplies sat near the inner wall. Two more Mussaurus hauled another pair of carts into the cave, then shrugged off their harnesses.

Squeak, Sniff, Snarfle, and Snorf bobbed their heads and ushered the group into the cave with high-pitched, singsong calls.

Lian had to concentrate to understand their peculiar way of speaking:

"Welcome you are!"

"Safe you will be!"

"This crisis will pass."

"What was is what will be."

As was the custom in her native China, Lian bowed to the gentle saurians to show respect. Her black silk robe flapped in the wind. Her long black hair did not move; it was bundled high and held in place with a wooden clip carved in the shape of a Skybax.

Lian felt the chill wind on her toes, revealed by her simple sandals. But she could also feel the pulsing cloud of heat rising from the fire.

She thought of the danger so many faced below. Clenching her fists in frustration, she winced at leaving the fight to others. A part of her wanted to leave now and join them.

But she knew it was wrong. And, taking a deep breath, she struggled with the warrior side of her nature.

Since she had washed up on the shore of Dinotopia as a young child, Lian had learned many things. The most amazing was learning about the love these humans and dinosaurs held for one another. It was unshakable. Within each of them resided a spirit far stronger and eternal than those flames raging below. To them, giving was the highest form of service.

And Lian knew that now was the time for her to give. Not fight.

She knew her young students were alone in the world, newly shipwrecked, as she had once been. And they were frightened. These "dolphinbacks" needed her.

Releasing her breath, Lian felt her calm return. She was ready.

"Everyone, if you're hungry, then eat, but remember we must make our supplies last," she announced.

Only a few were able to eat. Most looked far too worried. Lian knew what she had to do.

"Gather 'round," she said, hoping to keep them calm. "I have a story to tell all of you."

She waited as all her students and the four saurians assembled around her. Then she said, "This is a story of adventure. Of thrills and danger. And of explorers."

"Is this about the Knights of the Unrivaled?" a boy named Mishka asked eagerly. He pulled at his tunic and scratched an itch as he struggled to get comfortable on the hard cave ground.

Lian saw the light from one of the lanterns flicker on his round face, which was framed by curly blond locks.

"It is indeed," Lian said as she smiled warmly.

Murmurs of excitement rushed through the small gathering. She couldn't think of a single day when at least one of her students didn't ask for a tale about the Unrivaled, a tribe of brave Troodon knights.

Lian had become famous on the island for her role in finding this legendary "lost" tribe. Just two years ago, she and her friends had snuck into the forbidden lost city of Halcyon and, to their surprise, found a tribe of Troodons who had withdrawn from Dinotopian society centuries before.

It was Lian and her friends who convinced them to join Dinotopian society again.

"You said explorers," Kiki cried. She was a dark-haired girl with wide eyes. "Is it about the Explorers Club? About Plodnob and his friends?"

"I like Snicknik the quick," a young freckle-faced boy said.

"You would," the girl said. "Before you came here, *you* couldn't sit still, either!"

Lian studied the faces of her students, delighting in their excitement. Each had been raised in the human world outside Dinotopia. And each had faced difficulties learning the ways of the island, or coming to terms with the loss of loved ones or their feelings of loneliness. They had each learned so much and come so far.

All except Alec, a fair-haired lad who wore a weathered crimson shirt and dark leggings and boots. He had green eyes and a sour expression that hadn't changed in the weeks Lian had spent with him. He eyed the mouth of the cavern and looked ready to bolt at the first opportunity.

"This is a tale of the Explorers Club," Lian said. "But it is *not* a story from the past."

Her students looked to one another in confusion. Even Alec appeared mildly interested.

"What do you mean not from the past? The Explorers Club existed hundreds of years ago," Alec said. "Everyone knows that."

"But," Lian replied, "what few know is that each member of that club had descendants. Namesakes. And they're all about my age."

"That would make them squires," Alec said. His gaze finally drifted from the cave mouth. "Knights-in-training."

"Can this Seeno the stealthy tickle the nose of a sleeping sauropod and not wake him, just like his ancestor?" Mishka asked.

"And Snicknik!" the freckle-faced lad cried. "Can he outrace a storm, like the Snicknik that came before him?"

"I bet Plodnob the jovial could make even nasty old Lee Crabb laugh!" Kiki said.

"And Hardshell the strong could carry a young Diplodocus!" a dark-haired boy added.

Alec shrugged. "And Pointynog the clever could find a way to turn a Tyrannosaurus into a vegetarian. What of it?"

"That's just it," Lian said. "All their lives, these young explorers have felt as if they've had to measure up to the legends and legacies of their ancestors. They've felt a great responsibility—"

"The only responsibility any of us should feel is to ourselves," Alec cut in.

A hush fell upon the group. Suddenly, Alec was being pelted by crumbs and pillows.

"Enough!" Lian hollered. "Quite enough of that!"

The students drew away from Alec, whose bitter expression had returned. His gaze was now firmly fixed on the cave mouth.

"Fine," Alec said. "I'll keep my opinions to myself. I'm used to going it alone."

Squeak, Sniff, Snarfle, and Snorf rose up on their hind legs.

"Alone one may never be!"

"Surely that is plain to see."

"To roll far and wide from one's nest . . ."

"That can never, ever be best!"

Lian focused on the back of Alec's head.

"You can be by yourself," she told him, "even in a crowd of people. But on Dinotopia, you're only alone if you wish it."

Alec remained silent.

"On top of that," continued Lian, "it may surprise you to know that you're not the first dolphinback to come to this island and feel that way. At least for a time. But listen closely. Because I promise you, when this story is over, you will believe in the possibilities. And it's that belief that will save you, no matter what you may face."

Alec finally looked back to Lian.

"All right," he said. "Tell me."

CHAPTER 1

The race was an easy one for Snicknik. He took the lead in no time.

The mazelike route beneath the city's streets was difficult for most to navigate. But that was no surprise to Snicknik. The elder Troodon knights of Halcyon took the testing of their young knights-in-training very seriously. No challenge was simple.

Obstacles lay at every turn, and Snicknik leaped nimbly over them all, proving himself as graceful as the famous ancestor he'd been named after—Snicknik the quick!

More obstacles came Snicknik's way: a low pile of stones, a wagon, a cart, a sack of something or other. The young Troodon cleared every one. And then he stopped. He could have sworn that last one let out a moan.

It may have been nothing. But he wasn't about to ignore what might have been a cry for help. That wouldn't be knightly.

He turned and trotted back to the spot. There,

Snicknik found another member of the race lying on the ground.

"Spindletail?" Snicknik said. "What happened?"

"I've been here the last two laps," Spindletail said. "My ankle. It feels twisted. Would you help me to get out of here?"

Snicknik heard the sound of his fellow runners thundering closer. He was in the lead, but he wouldn't be much longer!

"I'll help you," Snicknik said.

He looked around the dim tunnel and saw a long support beam in the ceiling nearby. It was dangling and didn't look as if it was supporting much of anything, so Snicknik jumped up high and hit the beam with his snout.

It clattered to the cobblestones. Ignoring the dust and dirt falling onto his armor from above, Snicknik handed the wooden beam to the injured Troodon.

"There you are," Snicknik said. "You can use that as a crutch."

He helped Spindletail get to his one good foot and wedged the support beneath his other arm.

"Thank you," Spindletail said. "I thought no one would stop, no one would notice—"

"Quite welcome, quite welcome," Snicknik said briskly. Then he bounded forward to rejoin the race.

He was less than a dozen paces down the tunnel when he heard the support break. There was a thud and another low moan.

Sighing, Snicknik went back. He helped the wounded Troodon to his feet.

"Put your weight on me," Snicknik said.

"You'll help me to get out?" Spindletail asked.

"I'll help you," Snicknik said.

He was trying his best to be patient, but it wasn't one of his greatest virtues, as the sour Sir Jolley, his teacher, always reminded him.

Snicknik heard the heavy footfalls nearing. He saw dark shapes turn a corner at the end of the tunnel. Moving swiftly, Snicknik practically dragged Spindletail to a small crevice set in from the wall.

He made it there just in time. A furious rumble came, and a dozen blurred forms swept by them. Snicknik watched his fellow runners go. He still had a lap on them. The race was far from lost.

"I'll send for help the moment I cross the finish," Snicknik said.

Spindletail raised his hand. "But I thought—"

"Must fly," Snicknik said. "Bye-bye!"

The speedy dinosaur again broke into a run. But then another moan stopped him.

Unfortunately, this sound had not come from Spindletail. It came from farther down the tunnel. It was a deep but very loud moan that came just as the ceiling started to sag—right where he had removed the support!

"Oh, no," murmured Snicknik as the ceiling

sagged more and more. Then just above Spindletail's head, a section collapsed!

Snicknik raced back, moving in the fastest sprint of his life, and snatched the arm of his frightened fellow dinosaur. He hauled Spindletail to safety as a heavy chunk of debris smashed to the cobblestone and spat little stones toward them. Luckily, their armor gave them protection from the rain of stone and earth.

When the noise stopped, the ceiling seemed to have sunk as much as it was going to—only a few feet.

The runners came again. They narrowed into a single file to go around the rubble, and Snicknik and Spindletail flattened their flanks against the wall to avoid being trampled.

Snicknik got Spindletail to his feet, supporting most of his weight.

"Now you'll help me out of here?" Spindletail asked in a small, worried voice.

"Yes," Snicknik grumbled, knowing full well he had lost the race. "Now I'll help you out of here."

When it was over, Snicknik stood before Westwind, a twitchy dinosaur who seemed to have almost as much trouble standing still as Snicknik. Westwind wore silver armor and a crest shaped like wings.

Snicknik told him everything.

"You could have helped him to get out of the tunnel in the first place and still had time to win the race," Westwind said.

"I hadn't expected everything that happened to happen," Snicknik said.

Westwind shrugged. "Sometimes there's a quick way of doing a thing and then there's the right way. But the quick way, you'll often discover, takes twice the time because you must do one quick thing after another after another, and none of those things help. Because none of them are the *right* thing, which you'll end up doing anyway."

"That's why I lost the race," Snicknik said.

"Yes," Westwind said. "But you've won something greater."

"What's that?"

"Knowledge," Westwind said. "I, for one, will be curious to see what you do with it."

CHAPTER 2

Meanwhile, in another part of Halcyon, a different sort of test was taking place.

"Look at him," said a young dinosaur. "He may be as strong as his ancestor, but I'd wager he doesn't have the brains to know what to do with all his strength!"

Laughter came, and Hardshell felt crestfallen as he hurled the boulder toward the target. It was an underhanded throw, of course. The young Troodon's tiny arms were not capable of anything else with so great a weight. Even so, the boulder traveled eleven feet and landed just short of the mark set by Strongarm, the mammoth elder knight presiding over the tossing contest.

Hardshell shrank back as the young knight-in-training who had been teasing him bent low to pick up a boulder. That knight wore leather armor—only those members of the Unrivaled enduring the Punishment of Shame dressed that way. He had disgraced the steel that represented the strength and will of the Troodon knights.

Yet he acted as if he didn't care in the least.

"Let's see now," announced the leather-clad knight, "considering my size, which is considerably less than the lummox over there, I expect to do half as well. Precisely half!"

He took a step back, then made a mockery of his toss, sending the rock he had chosen high into the air. It landed with a thud midway between him and the boulder Hardshell had thrown.

Strongarm walked toward the target to study the rock's position. He was a huge Troodon dressed in black armor with crimson details.

"Five and a half feet," announced Strongarm. "You did half as well as Hardshell. Precisely. Very controlled. One cannot deny, an accomplished feat."

Hardshell's shoulders slumped.

The shamed knight laughed as he looked over at Hardshell. "What's wrong? You didn't have the brains to see that coming? Honestly, I'm not surprised."

Several of the knights who had gathered in the clearing outside the walls of Halcyon to witness Hardshell's final challenge nodded and laughed. The others rolled their eyes with disinterest.

Strongarm approached Hardshell. "You have but one way to prove yourself. Toss the next boulder precisely the same distance as the first one you threw. If it hits just right, it will split when it strikes the first stone. And it will prove your own control. That has only been done once before, Hardshell.

And I think you know who accomplished the feat."

Hardshell knew all too well. It had been his own famous ancestor, the one he'd been named after—Hardshell the strong.

"I'm ready," Hardshell said. He tried to keep the emotion out of his voice, but his body was tight and his hands trembled ever so slightly.

"As ready as a hatchling Iguanodon is to cross the Rainy Basin alone," the shamed knight muttered.

Hardshell heard the insult. He shook as he tossed the rock. It rose higher than he had desired and fell just short of the first boulder. A sigh came from those gathered.

"Oh, well," the shamed knight said. "I suppose this one never heard of flexing the muscles in his brains."

Laughter rang out. Turning on his opponent, Hardshell rushed toward the shamed Troodon. "Why are you saying these things? I don't even know you."

"And you probably never will. But it doesn't take much for someone like me to know all I need to know about you. And that is your failing."

With another laugh, the shamed knight walked away. The spectators slowly drifted away, and Strongarm approached the trembling Hardshell.

"I failed," Hardshell said.

"Nonsense," Strongarm replied. "You won. The contest was one of strength. And you tossed the rock farther than any of the other competitors. It was the shamed knight who turned it into a test of precision and control."

"Do you know that knight?" Hardshell asked. "The one who was making fun of me?"

"Of course," Strongarm said. "I'm the one that asked him to participate."

"Why him?" Hardshell asked. "He's earned the Punishment of Shame. Why someone so cruel?"

"Because a knight may not always be admired or even liked," Strongarm said. "And that is of little consequence when there is a task at hand. You must focus. Your emotions are relevant only when they do not interfere with your mission. Your responsibility lies in performing your knightly duties. For others. And for yourself. Until you find the strength to achieve that focus, you may never make your deepest and most cherished dreams a reality. And I believe you have it in you to do just that, but it will not come easily. Such things never do."

Hardshell stood alone as Strongarm went off with a handful of older knights. Then he crouched near the rock he had failed to split, picked up the second stone, and angrily hammered it down upon the first.

On the brink of becoming overwhelmed by his emotions, Hardshell found a quiet and dark corner near one of the city's entrances to be alone.

And to think.

CHAPTER 3

Deep within the dank lower reaches of the walled city of Halcyon, Seeno passed a long shadowy corridor.

All the torches along the wall had been extinguished. The only light came from the glowing green moss on the ceiling. But Seeno's sight was sharp, and he could see that he'd come to a special place—the Corridor of Time.

Paintings lined the walls. Each showed a scene of the greatest deeds ever performed by the Knights of the Unrivaled. And though he knew it was a foolish thing to do while he was being tested, Seeno hesitated for a moment to gaze at them.

As the lean-muscled young Troodon stole slowly down the corridor, he took great care that no step he took rang the bells or rattled the chains dangling from his armor. Even the slightest movement of air was counteracted to keep the chimes welded to his plates from tinkling.

The images on the wall told bold stories of Troodon knights facing angry tyrannosaurs, rescuing hatchlings from floods, and jousting with fierce Deinonychus in Raptortown.

Five images in particular stopped him.

The first was of a strongly built Troodon knight lifting a huge Diplodocus hatchling.

The great Hardshell the strong, thought Seeno with a smile.

The second painting was of a knight who was practically a blur as he outraced a dark, twisting wind.

The legendary Snicknik the quick . . .

The third was a beautiful rendering of a member of the Unrivaled sitting on a log beside a tyrannosaur whose mouth was stuffed with greens.

Seeno nodded, recognizing the much-admired *Pointynog the clever . . .*

The fourth was an image of a laughing Troodon knight standing between two groups of Deinonychus. The fierce groups wore the colors of rival tribes, yet the knight between them had them laughing together like brothers.

Plodnob the jovial, of course! thought Seeno.

And finally, the fifth painting was of a knight in armor much like Seeno's—only without the bells, chains, and chimes that had been affixed earlier for his test. The painting showed Seeno's ancestor tickling the nose of a sleeping sauropod with an Archaeopteryx feather.

My beloved namesake—Seeno the stealthy!

The feather in the painting reminded Seeno why

he was standing here in the first place.

He had been sent to snatch the feathered pen of Shakestail the scribe right out from under his snout. A difficult task, but Seeno had patience and a great deal of practice in the fine art of being invisible.

He had one other gift, too: the ability to detect flaws.

It might be a flaw in an object, a flaw in a plan, or even a flaw in a person. But this was a gift he kept to himself whenever possible because no one liked to hear about flaws!

Seeno was about to move along down the dark corridor when he heard an odd hissing sound. His curiosity roused, he stole ahead and saw a light flickering from a doorway.

Moving silently, he peered inside and saw a well-lit chamber in which Malthorpe the mirror master was toiling in his workshop.

Seeno liked mirrors very much. He was not a vain dinosaur. He simply appreciated fine craftsmanship, and he had always wanted to see Malthorpe actually create a mirror. For years, however, Seeno had simply been too shy to ask the dinosaur to let him observe.

Hmmm . . . thought Seeno. *Staying a few moments to get a closer look will only take a minute or two. What harm can it do?*

He slipped into Malthorpe's candlelit chamber. In and around the many worktables, there were dozens of mirrors of every shape and size.

With all the mirrors in this place, not getting spotted in here is quite the challenge, Seeno thought. *This alone would have made a greater final test for my rite of passage to knighthood.*

And he accomplished it easily, too!

He snuck around, darting silently from one spot to another as Malthorpe worked on a very large and oddly oblong mirror.

Seeno was careful to judge the angles of reflections in the many mirrors and to keep his image from appearing in any within Malthorpe's line of vision.

And all the while, Seeno watched the mirror master cool the surface of the low, plump mirror with a liquid Seeno didn't recognize. Malthorpe, a hunched-over Troodon with black and purple scales, nodded in satisfaction as he carefully checked to see that the mirror held no flaws.

At the same time, however, Seeno had to restrain a gasp. He could see a flaw in Malthorpe's creation. His keen gaze fixed on a hairline crack.

Now, that slim fissure might fill in as the glass hardened, leaving no flaw at all.

But Seeno knew it was more likely that the flaw would grow deeper and one day cause the mirror to shatter at a slight provocation. And that would be dangerous for whoever possessed the mirror.

Seeno didn't know what to do. It was certainly not his place to criticize a master craftsman, but his gift for detecting flaws had yet to fail him.

"Lord Botolf will be pleased," Malthorpe murmured to himself with pride. "We must always change, renew, rejuvenate ourselves; otherwise, we harden. And as he has changed, growing outward and to either side from his many joyous feasts, Lord Botolf will at last be able to see himself fully in this single large looking glass!"

Seeno's eyes widened as he realized the mirror was for Lord Botolf himself, the ruler of Halcyon!

Seeno knew that he had only a short time to act. Once the mirror's surface had fully hardened, there would be no correcting the mistake.

But the flaw might never appear, Seeno argued with himself. *A break might never result.*

Seeno wrestled with the possibilities until the moment had passed. The surface had hardened. It was too late to say a thing.

Seeno left the mirror master's chamber, turned the corner, and was surprised by a tap on the shoulder.

He didn't even hear Lightfoot's steps upon the cobbles as the older knight circled around from behind him. Lightfoot must have been in Malthorpe's chamber, too! The tall, lithe elder Troodon knight dressed all in black. The shadows were his second home.

"Sometimes *not* making a decision is the same as making one," Lightfoot said softly.

"What—what—" Seeno stuttered.

"The flaw," Lightfoot said. "I saw it, too. I'll tell

Malthorpe about if after we're done. He'll have to start over, but I think he would prefer that, considering the alternative."

Seeno hung his head. "I failed. I didn't retrieve the feather before you could catch me."

"I could have caught you at any time," Lightfoot said. "But I decided I had seen enough. As to whether or not you failed, I leave that up to you to decide."

They slipped down the corridor and were out of view of the mirror master before they spoke again.

"I could have said something about the flaw, but I was afraid of upsetting the master," Seeno said.

"It's true that sometimes it's a kindness not to point out a flaw," Lightfoot said. "But at other times, that silence can simply be a lack of willingness to take responsibility and can result in later and greater injury."

"But I've been told that wisdom has two parts," Seeno said. "Having a lot to say—and not saying it."

Lightfoot angled his head to one side. "Perhaps, in your case, it should be more a matter of having a lot to say and having the wisdom to know *when* to say it."

"How do I learn something like that?" Seeno asked.

"You live," the knight said. He clasped Seeno's shoulder and nodded. "That, my friend, is all it takes."

CHAPTER 4

Plodnob was never more jovial!

A group of young squires sat around him in a small chamber near the main library, listening to Plodnob tell silly stories for ten minutes. The young Plodnob hadn't yet failed to make his appreciative audience laugh.

This was too easy! thought Plodnob.

Luckily, his teacher had allowed him to choose his jovial nature as the virtue on which to be given his final test.

"And then, the thick plottens!" Plodnob said. "Because underneath all of his many disguises, the dinosaur was no bigger than a chicken!"

Snorts, chuckles, and more laughter greeted him.

As Plodnob glanced around the chamber, he realized that there were no windows.

With no elder knight in the room to observe, Plodnob suddenly wondered exactly how he would be judged.

Would it be a simple matter of quizzing the squires?

Plodnob's head started to hurt. *Too much thought!*

Suddenly, a rumbling came from somewhere in the chamber. It echoed from one wall to another, making it impossible to judge where it came from.

He patted his belly. "It wasn't me!"

The squires laughed, but a few appeared concerned. That concern grew as the rumbling came again, coupled with a shaking that rippled through Plodnob's entire body.

What is happening?!

"Squires, it comes to me that perhaps the time has come to take our fun elsewhere," Plodnob said, trying to remain calm.

Dust and dirt fell from the ceiling as the rumbling and shaking grew worse.

"I think it's an earthquake!" a thin squire with a crinkly snout cried.

"That would be as silly as a log on a bump-thump de dump!" Plodnob said. "Still, to the door, then. My cousin Pointynog is engaging in a great bit of entertaining business in the arena even as we speak, and, if you'd like, we can go visit him!"

The thin squire went to the door and yanked at its handle. But it didn't budge!

Plodnob tried the door himself. But it was truly stuck. He rapped on it and called out to anyone in the outer hall, but there was no reply.

"How about up there?" the thin squire said as he pointed to a staircase in the chamber that led to a high door.

The rumbling and shaking continued. The squires had to duck and leap as bits of stone fell around them.

"Up there it is, smart lad!" Plodnob said as he turned from the door. He didn't see the two squires who had bent low to check the door's hinges—until he tripped over them!

Plodnob's fall brought laughter to the squires, but that was cut short as more rubble fell from above.

Panicked cries began as Plodnob tried to get to his feet, but the squires kept stepping onto his back in their confusion. Some headed toward the stairs, others away from them.

With a great bellow, Plodnob pushed himself up, scattering several of the squires.

"To the stairs!" the thin squire said as he directed those he could toward the upper door.

Plodnob couldn't see if it was open or not from where he stood, but he knew he had to get these squires to safety.

"Listen to him now," Plodnob said. "Have a-whaaahhh!"

Plodnob slipped on a pair of stray stones and fell full on his big round bottom. The panicked squires couldn't help but take note of the pratfall, with several laughing despite the danger they faced.

"Wait for me, lads!" Plodnob shouted as he

SAGINAW CHIPPEWA ACADEMY
LIBRARY MEDIA CENTER
MT. PLEASANT, MI 48858

attempted to rise. "Plodnob might be quick with a comeback, but he's sometimes a little slow on his feet."

The squires didn't wait for him. Nor did they listen when he told them not to crowd the foot of the staircase and to ascend one at a time. They pressed against one another, and only a handful got out of the room through the door above before the rumbling finally ended.

"All right, all right," the thin squire said in a suddenly much deeper and authoritative voice. "Single file, all of you."

The squires lined up, just as they had been commanded.

"Now leave us," the squire said. "Plodnob and I must chat."

Plodnob was startled as he watched the squires happily ascend the stairs. Several were repeating his jokes and jests, and that lifted his heart.

But . . .

Plodnob turned to the thin "squire." He looked closely at the Troodon and noticed the little scar running across his snout.

"Jaggedsnout!" Plodnob said. "Why, I didn't recognize you out of full armor, and surrounded by those squires."

"I know, and more's the pity," Jaggedsnout said. The little knight shook his head. "They must do more than be amused by you, Plodnob. They must *respect* you. If you have learned any lesson today, I hope it is that one."

Plodnob waited until the knight had gone with the squires, then he bent down and picked up a chunk of the debris that had fallen from the ceiling. It was harmless, made of paper and soft cloth.

"A fine jest!" Plodnob said. "Truly!"

But no one was there to listen.

CHAPTER 5

Pointynog the clever squinted in the harsh sunlight as he stared at the field of battle.

He'd begun this fight with twenty Troodon knights to command. Now only four remained. His opponent, however, had more than a dozen warriors left.

"What is your move?" Ripclaw the bold demanded.

Pointynog stiffened. He had been playing chess all of his life. He loved the game and all the possibilities it presented. Countless strategists had devised one manner of play after another over the centuries on Dinotopia. Pointynog had studied all the theories of the greatest.

And yet—he was losing.

"Honor demands that you answer me," Ripclaw said. "If you do not, then you will forfeit this game."

Pointynog made his move.

Seconds after he spoke, two warriors met in mock combat, performing a ritualized dance that mimicked the motions of true combat. Then one fell.

Pointynog looked to his opponent. Ripclaw, a fabulously tall and quick-witted knight who wore a crimson sash, made his move without hesitation. Pointynog winced as his warrior fell.

The crowd of spectators in the great arena gasped.

Pointynog could think of only one thing to do now. Speaking with a boldness he did not truly feel, Pointynog gave the orders and maneuvered his remaining warriors into the endgame. He lost one more piece, but that didn't matter.

Six moves later, their judge, the chess master Ironjaw the mighty, nodded solemnly. "A stalemate. I declare this match a draw."

There was no applause. Instead, his opponent Ripclaw approached and held out his claws. They were covered by shiny silver gauntlets.

Pointynog reached out and the knight drew him into a warrior's embrace. He struck Pointynog's back so hard with his friendly enthusiasm that the brilliant young strategist was certain he would find dents in his armor later.

"Well played," Ripclaw said as he pulled away.

"I don't understand," Pointynog said. "I used every trick I've ever learned, but you would have beaten me anyway. It's not that you're smarter than me, or the better player, so what happened?"

Ripclaw's upper lips lifted a little. He drew his ceremonial blade, which had not been sharpened in decades. "Lad, I think you should have chosen tact as the virtue to be tested in this final challenge. For someone so clever, you're as blunt as my sword."

"Honest and true," Pointynog said. "Both your words—and mine."

With a sigh, Ripclaw turned and walked away.

Ironjaw approached. "I overheard your question and can answer it simply. Ripclaw wasn't playing to win. His strategy was to force you into a situation in which you would become *convinced* that you would not win. You see, he knew that if you felt you would lose, then you would evade defeat by going for the stalemate. And so you did."

"He wasn't playing to win?" Pointynog said. "What manner of foolishness is that? What point is there to any contest other than winning or losing?"

Ironjaw stared at the young knight. "Some solutions are simple. Overcomplicating a situation often leads to confusion and failure. If you had seen through what was really happening, you would have been able to see the way to win."

"So this was a trick," Pointynog said.

"It was a reflection of something you might face in life. And, remember, not every game can be won."

"Right," Pointynog said. "A trick. But this will not stop me from being declared a knight at last, a squire no longer."

"Of course," Ironjaw said. "This round of 'trials' is largely ceremonial. A knight you shall be. But the *kind* of knight . . . well, that is something that can only be decided in a contest with yourself. Perhaps you should engage in one. You might find the results . . . interesting."

"I'll consider it," Pointynog said.

Ironjaw bowed to Pointynog with a flourish reserved for one knight paying respect to another.

It was a moment Pointynog would have cherished more if not for the somewhat troubling words of the judge.

But he did enjoy it, nonetheless.

A knight clad in armor painted a perfect, pristine ivory stood near the exit from the arena. Sir Jolley watched as Pointynog's family rushed onto the field to embrace their son.

Likewise, the ivory knight's other four charges emerged from their various tests and met their loved ones on the field.

Sir Jolley felt a certain sadness as he watched his students. After today, these five would be squires no longer. They would be addressed as knights, and they would no longer be his to tutor and train. Though they had been a difficult lot, he would miss them.

Each had been less of a disappointment than he had expected, and in his life, that was rare. Of course, it was easier to understand a thing like that in hindsight. Now that his time with these young squires was over, he could relax a bit. Maybe he'd go on a trip around the island—take in the operas of Waterfall City, or see the new marvels in the Denison Studio . . .

The sound of a throat clearing brought the spotlessly attired knight back from his musings. Sir Jolley looked up in surprise at Dragonhorn, messenger to Lord Botolf himself. His fellow knight was dressed in traditional steel grays, with marks and splotches and cracks and dents marring his armor.

Sir Jolley shuddered inwardly. Many knights considered such blemishes badges of honor. Just like—horrible as it was to contemplate—scars gained in knightly service.

Only a single light blue sash around Dragonhorn's middle and an image of the Kraken, Lord Botolf's totem, chiseled into his breastplate, gave the knight's look even a flair of distinction.

"Lord Botolf wants to see you," Dragonhorn said.

Sir Jolley tensed. "The reason?"

"It's about your students . . ."

CHAPTER 6

Sir Jolley entered the throne room silently, his head hung low.

Lord Botolf's legendary girth seemed to have increased since the last time Sir Jolley had seen the great leader. Some of his armored bulk actually seemed to hang over the sides of the three-foot-wide stone throne.

Jolley stepped closer, and when he finally saw the stern look on Lord Botolf's face, he tried not to shake within his ivory armor.

The huge Troodon was staring at him with such fury and wrath that Jolley felt entirely like a fool. His students had shortcomings, there was no doubt. And as their teacher, he would be the one to take the blame.

Jolley could hardly stand the look on Botolf's face. The tension alone nearly brought him to the point of weeping for forgiveness. He was about to open his snout when Botolf spoke first. But it wasn't a language Jolley readily recognized.

Jolley listened again, for another phrase. It was a strange, snarfling language. It was—

Snoring.

Lord Botolf had fallen asleep with his eyes open!

"Lord Botolf?" Sir Jolley called gently. Then more forecefully. "Lord Botolf!"

With a start, the gigantic Troodon shook himself awake. He blinked several times and cleared his throat.

"Ah!" Lord Botolf said. "Sir Jolley! Good of you to come."

"Is it?" Sir Jolley asked, his voice nearly cracking from the strain he felt.

"Of course!" Lord Botolf said. "Unless you'd rather be somewhere else?"

Sir Jolley dropped to one knee with a clank of his armor. "No, Lord Botolf, most esteemed and exalted one. I live to serve in whatever minute and minuscule way I might."

Lord Botolf leaned forward. He appeared perplexed. "What?"

"Only that I wish to please and express my acceptance and gratitude of your every whim and willy-nilly way of wonder, that is all," Sir Jolley said nervously.

"Ah, yes. I see," Lord Botolf said. He looked around the vast chamber, a low rumbling sigh making his snout wiggle. "I would assume you're curious about my slumber?"

Sir Jolley rose to his feet. His tail itched. His tail

always itched when he had no idea what someone was talking about.

"That is exactly what was on my mind," Sir Jolley managed to reply.

"As well it should be!" Lord Botolf roared. "Some of our greatest advisers have told me that we learn when we sleep. Our minds digest information and allow us to reach conclusions in this state. And so I have given to napping whenever a great decision must be made."

Sir Jolley opened his hands and looked to the ceiling. "If you are making them, they must be of a righteous and unspeakably exalted, illustrious, and imposing nature."

Lord Botolf strained his neck as he followed Sir Jolley's gaze. "Is there something up there?"

Sir Jolley returned his gaze to Lord Botolf. "Only if you so wish it."

Lord Botolf scratched the side of his scaly head. "Listen now. Carefully. Try to understand."

The ivory-clad knight nodded. "Unfruitably."

"There is a task," Lord Botolf said. "A simple matter that needs to be done. The dolphins have saved another drowning traveler and deposited him upon our Dinotopian shores. The lad must be escorted from a village not far from here."

"Which village?" asked Jolley.

"Doondawdle."

"And escorted where?"

"To a dock near the Black Fish Tavern," answered Lord Botolf, "and then to the Festival of Understanding at the Serpentine Cathedral on the Outer Island."

"What is the dolphinback's name?"

"Nicholas. He must be seen by the Tribunal of Understanding, which meets only at that festival, and the date of his appointment is two weeks from today, just before nightfall. If he is late, the Tribunal will have no choice but to make a very important decision that may impact his future—and all without benefit of meeting him or hearing what he has to say. That would be a grave thing, indeed."

"Unquestionably," Sir Jolley said.

"For this reason, I wish to send a very select group of knights," Lord Botolf said.

"And you wish me to be among them?" Sir Jolley asked brightly.

"More than that," Lord Botolf said. "I wish you to advise them. To help and inspire them."

Sir Jolley felt overwhelmed. "You wish me for this honor?"

"Who else?" Lord Botolf said. "The five knights I've chosen are, after all, your students."

Sir Jolley gagged. He sputtered and almost spat.

"You wish for *my students* to be this boy's escort?" Sir Jolley asked. He was aghast. "You want Plodnob and his companions to take this lad through the Rainy Basin and then on a sailing ship rounding half the island?"

"With you accompanying them, of course," Lord Botolf said. The big-bellied Troodon sat back on his throne. He looked very satisfied. "It all came to me in my dreams. A wonderful thing, dreams. They keep the heart alive."

"But, unequivocally, I have duties and responsibilities," Sir Jolley said. "And my students' status as knights is prevalently neoteric. I could meditate, ruminate, muse, and ponder, but I should hardly think them ready—"

"Are you challenging my judgment and wisdom?" Lord Botolf roared.

"Most esteemed you are in your rotunditude," Sir Jolley said quickly. "Of this, there can be no doubt."

The huge, round Troodon settled back in his throne. His claws clicked on its stone arms. "Just so long as we're clear on that."

"Verifiably," Sir Jolley said.

"Now bring in your students," Lord Botolf said.

"My apologies. But their whereabouts are not meticulously matriculated at all times to the best of my considerably extendible awareness," Sir Jolley said.

"I had them summoned after you. They should be right outside."

"Ah," Sir Jolley said. "Yes."

He marched to the chamber's double doors and opened them. All five of his "brave young explorers" waited in the hallway. He ushered them inside and stood behind them as they approached Lord Botolf.

"Is it true you fought the Kraken?" Pointynog the clever asked. "I always thought it was a figure of myth."

"I fought it on the only battlefield that matters," Lord Botolf said. "The one where hearts and minds and imagination lead us to our destiny."

"Right," Pointynog said. He nodded as if making a mental note. "I didn't think so."

Sir Jolley was about to scold Pointynog, but Lord Botolf held up a single gauntleted hand to stop him.

"There are many ways to look at a thing, young knight," said Botolf.

"Really?" Pointynog said. "I prefer to look in the general direction of where my head is pointed. The whole 'corner of the eye' business just gives me eyestrain."

Lord Botolf narrowed his gaze, and then he sat back, laughing heartily. "I have made the right choice!"

Pointynog glanced at his friends. "There's *choosing* going on here? No one told me about choosing."

"Choosing how? Or who? Or where or when?" asked Snicknik the quick. He spoke very fast, his words a sudden rush. He danced in place, as he always did. "What is it we are supposed to choose?"

"You are not choosing, young knight. You have been chosen," Lord Botolf said. Then he explained just what their mission would be.

"I'll carry the boy the whole way on my back if

need be!" pronounced Hardshell the strong.

"I'll sneak him right past those hungry T. rexes," added Seeno the stealthy.

"And I'll keep him laughing the whole way there!" vowed Plodnob the jovial.

"Just get him there *on time*," Lord Botolf said. "Nothing more is required than that."

"What is this lad like?" Pointynog asked. "Where did he come from?"

"It is a very unusual situation," Lord Botolf said. "Yes, most unusual indeed. You know of the many shipwrecks that have brought dolphinbacks to our shores over the centuries. In this case, there was no shipwreck. Indeed, this poor lad says that he walks in his sleep, and that he fell from his ship in the middle of the night."

"How did he make it here?" Pointynog asked.

Plodnob nodded eagerly. "I love tales of adventure and heroism. How did he survive at all?"

"You'll be able to ask him yourself tomorrow," Lord Botolf said. "For now, rest and enjoy yourselves. The work of true knights lies ahead for all of you."

The explorers cheered. They turned and nearly toppled Sir Jolley as they rushed past him to the door.

Sir Jolley saw Lord Botolf's messenger standing in the doorway. He sighed and made one final appeal.

"Lord Botolf, they're only lads!" Sir Jolley said. "Immature and not immaculate, innocent but not necessarily inventive, all of which is indicative of indecision and incorrectness, not that I would presume to judge, for judiciousness is not my strong suit; however—"

The snoring stopped him. Lord Botolf's eyes were open, but he was clearly sound asleep once more. Sir Jolley sighed and left the chamber, his head hung low, his armor clinking sadly.

Dragonhorn, Lord Botolf's messenger, watched him go, then lightly stepped inside and closed the door.

"He's gone," Dragonhorn said inside the closed chamber.

Lord Botolf immediately stopped snoring. He didn't bother to blink or make a show of being awake this time. "That knight is such a toady."

"I wouldn't presume to argue," Dragonhorn said. "Not on that point. But I do worry that these lads aren't ready. I watched their final trials."

"They succeeded in their tasks, didn't they?" Lord Botolf asked.

"In the strictly literal sense, they did," Dragonhorn said. "But, as you pointed out, there is more than one way to look at a thing."

Lord Botolf waved his massive claw, as if ushering away the entire line of reasoning.

"This is a simple task," Lord Botolf said. "What could possibly go wrong?"

CHAPTER 7

At dawn the next day, Pointynog and his friends left Halcyon for the first time in over a year. They traveled in a carriage drawn by a fast-moving gray-and-purple-striped Tenontosaurus named Beatfeet.

Pointynog sat with Snicknik on a resting couch high above the carriage, where a driver might have sat, if Beatfeet hadn't already known the area so well.

Their bags and supplies were roped down behind them. Every now and then, Sir Jolley would poke his head out of the carriage to complain about the noise Snicknik was making, but otherwise, little was heard from the knights down below.

For most of the morning, Snicknik ran alongside the carriage and even gained on the swiftly moving Beatfeet, but it was difficult for him to run and chat at the same time. So when he wanted to talk, he slowed down and hopped up to join Pointynog.

"Festivals are indeed a very wonderful thing," Beatfeet said. "How could one get on without them?"

"It's more than that," Snicknik said. His tapping

tail and clicking claws betrayed his excitement. "We're knights at last! And this is our first mission!"

The ride soon became bumpy, and the passengers were jostled as they passed through a low range of mountains to the east, avoiding the Mudnest Trail completely. The grand, golden peaks of the mountains rose on either side of the carriage as Beatfeet raced to make their rendezvous.

They reached the outskirts of Doondawdle in time for lunch, and Beatfeet called out words of friendly greeting to a pair of armored Apatosaurus. They were waiting to carry the group through the Rainy Basin.

Each of the longnecks was seventy feet long and wore enormous saddles on its back. Huge stocks of supplies and hooks for hanging bags could be seen upon the saddles, along with high resting couches and lumpy canvas bags bearing presents and other items scheduled for delivery in Bonabba, Horsetail Grove, and Sauropolis.

Beside the two Apatosaurus stood a fresh-faced, dark-haired boy.

"That must be Nicholas," guessed Pointynog.

And beside Nicholas stood another Troodon.

"Ironjaw?" Pointynog was surprised to see the judge from the chess match the previous day.

Beatfeet halted the cart and the Troodon group jumped out. Sir Jolley looked a little sickly as he wobbled forward. The rest of the young knights collected their supplies from the roof of the carriage and came to join their former teacher.

"It would be fun, so much fun, to journey further with you," Snicknik said to Beatfeet.

"Another time," Beatfeet said. "The Rainy Basin is not for me. Those who dwell in that place have no sense of humor!"

With that, the Tenontosaurus was off, his unburdened carriage hopping and practically flying into the air behind him as he broke into a run toward the Golden Mountains.

Pointynog and the others waited for Sir Jolley to approach Ironjaw and the boy, but he shook his head.

"Undutifully I regard this chore a delight for you to suffer and smile through," he said. "Knights you wanted to be, so then you are, here, now, all that. Go!"

Pointynog took the lead at once. He approached the chess master with his friends trailing behind him. Only Snicknik broke from the group, racing off to introduce himself to the longnecks.

"Strength and honor!" Pointynog called out.

Ironjaw bowed to the younger knight. "Strength and honor! With your leave, I would accompany you as far as the Black Lizard Dock."

With my leave? Pointynog thought. *Well, now, I could get used to this!*

"The pleasure is ours," Pointynog said, raising his

snout in a mild challenge. "Are you to be another adviser, like Sir Jolley?"

Ironjaw's gaze did not leave Pointynog's. It was firm and unyielding. "I'm certain my presence can be of value, but I'm making this trip because I have business of my own at the docks."

Pointynog bowed. The situation was clear. This mission was his own to command. Ironjaw was not making a bid for supremacy.

As the caravan prepared to depart, Plodnob wobbled toward the pair. He nodded at Nicholas. "Fair lad, how fare you?"

"Well and honorably met," Nicholas said. "I have heard only good things about each of you and am anxious to know you better."

"The boy knows the social graces," Seeno said.

"Oh, and much more," Nicholas assured him. "You are explorers, one and all, are you not? And knights? True knights? How wonderful and fascinating!"

Plodnob blushed inwardly. "It is true that sometimes we impress even ourselves."

"I have no doubt," Nicholas said.

Pointynog looked around. "Isn't anyone coming to see you off?"

Nicholas laughed. "All good-byes have been said, all pleasantries exchanged."

"Then it is time we departed," Pointynog said.

Nicholas and Sir Jolley climbed up to a high

mount upon the nearest of the longnecks.

Pointynog studied the caravan in confusion. He turned to Ironjaw. "There doesn't seem to be room for all of us to ride. And it's odd. I thought there would be Styracosaurus escorts."

"*We* are the escorts," Ironjaw said. He gestured to a long rectangular box set near the footrest of the closest saurian saddle. "With your leave?"

"Please," Pointynog said.

Ironjaw opened the box, revealing shining lances and glittering shields. He handed a large silver lance to the young knight.

Pointynog took the lance, gauging its weight. Its point was dulled, but the steel shimmered and glinted in the bright sunlight. "Oh."

The group quickly set off. They headed south, eating on the way, and soon found themselves in the lush green reaches of Slumberbund Valley.

"This sounds like an exciting adventure," Nicholas called from his high perch. "I've been all over Dinotopia's mainland, but never to the Outer Island. I have to admit, I'm a little nervous at the thought of being on a boat again, considering what happened to me the last time."

"Hmmm," Pointynog said. "Perhaps one of us should keep watch over Nicholas each night."

"A sound idea," Ironjaw said merrily.

A coughing and something that might have been grousing came from above.

"After all," Ironjaw continued, "with his sleepwalking affliction, he might cause all manner of mischief and not even be aware of it."

"Very considerate of you," Nicholas called. His tone was flat.

Beside him, Sir Jolley moaned and held his stomach. He clearly wasn't happy with the modes of travel that had been chosen for them.

Pointynog and Ironjaw walked ahead of the others.

"That lad is certainly facing a dilemma," Pointynog said.

Ironjaw tensed. "What do you mean?"

"Walking in his sleep," Pointynog said. "What did you think I meant?"

The more experienced dinosaur shook his head. "I—I wasn't sure."

Pointynog thought Ironjaw's reaction strange, but he chose not to comment on it.

"Yes, to walk in one's sleep," Pointynog said. "To wake in strange places, in the midst of unusual events . . . I wonder if what a sleepwalker does is related to underlying thoughts and wishes. Lord Botolf says we deal with issues that are troubling us and reach conclusions about them when we slumber. I read a scroll on the subject."

"You make it sound as if a sleepwalker could somehow be responsible for his actions," Ironjaw said.

Pointynog held his lance high. "Dreams are strange things. And I acknowledge all possibilities."

"As well you should," Ironjaw said cryptically.

Pointynog slowed so that the others could catch up. Then he looked up to Nicholas.

"Nicholas, when you sleepwalk, what do you dream?" Pointynog asked.

Nicholas turned away uncomfortably. "I don't dream. Not ever."

"We all have our dreams," Plodnob said. "But you know what they say: Dreams come a size too big so we can grow into them!"

"Perhaps," Nicholas said.

"But what do I know?" Plodnob said merrily. "As they say, you are only as wise as others perceive you to be. And that hardly makes me a keeper of wisdom!"

Nicholas laughed at the larger Troodon's words. "I doubt that. I can tell already that you have untapped virtues—and unlimited potential."

Plodnob thanked Nicholas for the compliment. Only Pointynog wondered if Nicholas might have meant something less cheerful by his comment. The tone seemed almost threatening.

Pointynog's gaze narrowed on the boy. There was something not quite right about him. He had no idea what it might be, but he was certain he could figure it out, so long as he had enough time.

Soon, the clearings dwindled, and the paths between the great forests became more narrow. The firm ground turned damp, dank, and swampy. Clusters of tall trees with overhanging branches hid the sun and cast a gloom on the path, and mud and muck splattered the knights as they walked dutifully just ahead of the caravan.

Pointynog commanded Snicknik to put his restless energy and great speed to work circling the caravan, thus ensuring that they would have fair warning if a hungry pack of Tyrannosaurus decided to engage them.

"I am grateful to the core that I don't have to be down there!" Sir Jolley said, putting a proud claw to his spotless ivory-colored armor. "How sloppy and slovenly!"

Pointynog and Ironjaw again walked some distance ahead of the other knights. Ironjaw spoke very softly, so no one else would hear: "I wonder if you are aware that many in Halcyon have been perplexed by your training."

"What perplexes them?" asked Pointynog.

"That the care and training of the descendants and namesakes of our greatest knights fell to one such as Sir Jolley. Is it something the five of you ever take time to contemplate?"

Pointynog frowned. "I think Sir Jolley was given the task because no one else wanted it. Imagine, being known as the knight who failed to properly train the namesakes of Halcyon's five greatest knights."

"You feel as if you haven't received your due?"

Ironjaw said. "That your training has been lacking?"

"No," Pointynog said. "Actually, I don't. We have more to learn, of course, but any knight may say that."

"Very true," Ironjaw said. "But honestly, do you think that training the five of you is a duty a teacher might shirk?"

"I don't know," Pointynog said. "I might. I've heard people whisper that it was considered a great responsibility. But Sir Jolley has never treated us any differently than any of his other students, at least, by all accounts from some of his students that we've met."

From far above, Sir Jolley's raised voice drifted to the knights.

"Bugs and mud and crawling things that buzz and fly but do not thud!" The elder knight then wiped his ivory armor with the silk cloth he carried.

Ironjaw scratched his snout. "Sir Jolley may be a bit of a character," he admitted, "but in rules of etiquette and knowledge of culture and fair play, one must admit that few are known to surpass him."

"True," said Pointynog. "And consider . . . the final tests the five of us faced yesterday. We may have named the virtues to be tested, but Sir Jolley devised the rest. And I dare say we all learned from them."

"That is good," Ironjaw said with a nod. "And as to his odd manner of speech, well . . . when was being unique anything but a virtue on Dinotopia?"

"Wise words," Pointynog said. "Wise indeed."

Ironjaw hefted his shield. "Still, you seem troubled."

Pointynog looked around. "I've never crossed the Rainy Basin this way."

"What way is that?" Ironjaw asked.

Pointynog gestured at the bog. "On foot."

"I thought you were going to say as a knight. You've achieved your dream. The first part of it, anyway. Why not enjoy the mysteries?"

"Mysteries annoy me," Pointynog said. "I like plain and simple facts."

"All right, then—Fact one: We will not be walking the entire way . . . Fact two: There is a good reason we are walking now and an equally good reason we won't be walking later . . . And Fact final: If you were more observant, you would already know that reason."

Pointynog was puzzled. He wanted to ask more questions, but he knew his companion was testing him. He had given him clues, and now was the time to examine his surroundings and figure out what he had missed.

He studied the two longnecks tramping nearby. Each thud of their massive, elephant-like feet caused huge sprays of gunk and smelly water to splash around them. Their undersides were coated and dripping with the stuff.

Pointynog sniffed. The water did have a foul smell to it. Almost like—

The young knight whirled in alarm. "This water, it's more than collected rainfall, isn't it? Some of it has come from Tyrannosaurus!"

"Well," Ironjaw said. "They have to *go* somewhere. And so long as we have their scent on us, stinky as it is, we have a better chance of making it through this area with fewer encounters, in any case."

"Fewer?" Pointynog asked anxiously. "Why do you say *fewer*? That indicates a distressing inevitability. It suggests—"

Then he heard heavy thumps in the distance. They had gone unnoticed until now because their rhythm had been similar to the hulking, thunderous impacts of the gigantic longneck strides.

Now there was discord.

Flying feet.

The sounds grew louder.

Suddenly, Snicknik burst from a grove of trees and came racing their way. "They're big, they're not happy, and they're very, very *big*!"

Trees fell to the left of the caravan and the knights hurried into a line to face the threat.

A trio of crimson-and-black-skinned predators appeared. Their slavering maws opened wide.

Pointynog stared up at the darting tongues and teeth the size of daggers. Their eyes were bright with excitement and hunger.

RHHHHHRRR-AHHHRRRGGGHHH!

The Tyrannosaurus clan had arrived.

CHAPTER 8

"This is your mission, Pointynog," Ironjaw said in a cold, steely voice. "How will you lead?"

For the first time in his life, Pointynog's mind was blank. He stared at the rippling muscle and gargantuan forms of the three Tyrannosaurus and had no idea what to do. A terror unlike any he had ever faced overwhelmed him.

"I thought you said you had crossed the Rainy Basin before?" Ironjaw asked.

"Once," Pointynog whispered as the carnivores slowly approached. "I rode on a high perch like Sir Jolley and Nicholas. I heard a few rexes growling and roaring, but the predators weren't hungry or feeling up to a challenge that day."

"Perhaps I could offer some advice, as I have experience in these matters," Ironjaw said.

"Gah," Pointynog said, eyes wide.

"I'll take that as a yes," Ironjaw said. He raised his lance and boldly strode up to the Tyrannosaurus trio. A black-and-crimson-scaled T. rex stepped out in front of his companions to meet the knight.

Bowing to the dinosaur, Ironjaw spread his arms, aiming his shield in one direction, the lance in another. His breastplate and face were completely exposed.

The rex lunged, his jaws snapping. Ironjaw leaped back, narrowly avoiding the predator's attack. He smacked the Tyrannosaurus on the snout with his lance and fended off another rush of the rex's jaws with his shield.

"Sh-shouldn't we be h-helping him?" Plodnob stammered.

Pointynog just stood there, watching with all the rest. The pair of longnecks were nervously watching the battle. The other two Tyrannosaurus kept their distance.

"Don't so much as raise your lances unless the others come into this!" Ironjaw shouted. He jabbed and thrust with the lance, the rex always managing to avoid any direct blows. "We're in their home. Respect must be shown."

Suddenly, the Tyrannosaurus paused. He gave an inquisitive snorf.

As if in response, Ironjaw drew a long wavering line in the air.

From his perch, Sir Jolley said, "Roughly translated, 'Eels again? The last three convoys brought eels. Don't you have anything else?' "

Below, Pointynog's mental fog finally cleared. "It's

a ritual!" he softly exclaimed to the others. "An ancient ritual of greeting and respect between former enemies."

"Hah!" Nicholas called. "So this is just a formality. There's no real danger!"

Pointynog shuddered. "I didn't say—"

Before the young knight could finish his statement, Nicholas leaped out of his seat and slid down the sauropod's side. He rolled as he hit the ground, then surged forward and snatched up a shiny staff from the astounded Plodnob, who had been holding the instrument of defense very loosely.

Nicholas crossed directly between Ironjaw and the T. rex and poked the staff in the direction of the gigantic meat-eater.

"*En garde,* you ridiculous brute!" Nicholas hollered.

The predator's jaws swept down and flashed over Nicholas's head as Ironjaw leaped and knocked him out of the way.

"I thought this was a game!" Nicholas said.

"Not a game," Ironjaw said. "Never that."

The precise movements of the ritual dance of greeting had been disrupted. It was a high breach of etiquette, an irresponsible show of absolute disrespect.

With a roar, the rex who had been "jousting" with Ironjaw drove himself at the downed duo with a fury!

His claws raked muddy, gaping furrows in the

earth to either side of the muck-spattered pair. The other two Tyrannosaurus finally moved into action, surging ahead to attack the armored longnecks.

"They have to be stopped!" Pointynog called.

Snicknik was the quickest to act. He raced toward one of the rexes, planted his lance in the ground, and used it to vault into the air. He struck the side of the predator's head with a jarring impact that drove the carnivore back.

Dropping like a stone, Snicknik fell to the mud with a splash. He scrambled to his feet as the Tyrannosaurus lunged forward, attempting to fasten his jaws upon the young knight. Snicknik bolted and the angered predator raced after him, the pair blurring past the caravan as they headed deep into the woods.

As Ironjaw was joined by Hardshell to drive back the first Tyrannosaurus, the remaining rex headed right for the Apatosaurus who was hauling Sir Jolley!

Plodnob and Seeno moved to intercept that dinosaur, while above, Sir Jolley found that his tingling legs had fallen asleep. He was helpless— and trapped!

Pointynog acted swiftly on an idea, leaping onto the running board of the huge saddle slung over the longneck's back.

With another hop, he was near the crates containing the smoked eels they had carried along for just such an encounter. Pointynog clawed open the closest crate and dug in for a handful of the richly seasoned fish, but they were slippery, nearly impossible to grip. He could snatch up a few in his mouth, but that wouldn't be enough to make his plan a success.

His friends kept the predator busy as he tried to figure out what to do.

A low-lying leaf the size of his head brushed against his shoulder. Pointynog turned, and inspiration came to him once more. With his teeth and his claws, Pointynog cut loose several large leaves and used them to create a large scoop. With the leaves, he was able to dig out dozens of eels and wrap them for safe transport.

Then he scrambled down and raised the fish. The rex who was snapping at Plodnob and Seeno suddenly looked distracted. His nostrils flared, and he sniffed loudly.

"Come on, don't tell me you're not hungry!" Pointynog said.

The Tyrannosaurus roared and raced after Pointynog.

Fear returned to the young knight as he darted away from the caravan. He remembered seeing a deep mud bog a hundred feet off. If he could reach it, he might be able to trap the predator in its depths.

Unfortunately, he was running forward but looking back, and because he wasn't looking where he was going, his foot was snared in a tangle of roots. With a grunt, he slammed face-first into the muddy ground. The smelly eels flew over his head and landed a few feet past him.

Turning onto his back, Pointynog tried to free himself, but his leg was caught fast. The Tyrannosaurus continued to thunder toward him. Pointynog saw the massive jaws of the slavering Tyrannosaurus as the dinosaur sped his way. He kicked at the roots, but he couldn't break their hold. He was trapped!

Then the Tyrannosaurus was upon him. The young knight saw the predator's curved, spikelike teeth, his moist pink tongue. Pointynog squeezed his eyes shut. He felt the carnivore's breath, a fiery wind in his face, then he heard the terrible chomp as the rex's jaws slammed together.

Only—he didn't feel anything.

And he didn't hear the rending of his armor.

Opening his eyes, the young knight saw the blubbery black-and-crimson underside of the rex's neck shaking above him. Then he felt the ground tremble as a second Tyrannosaurus approached, and suddenly, hands and claws were upon him, freeing his trapped leg.

With an *ooomph* of effort, he was dragged out from under the feasting dinosaur and helped to his feet by Plodnob and Seeno. Ironjaw stood nearby, a pale-looking Nicholas at his side.

Pointynog turned to see the hungry rex stuffing

himself with the leaf-wrapped eels. Huge fronds stuck out from between his teeth, and it looked as if he had just munched on a nearby tree. The second rex munched on the eels that had been missed by the first.

"I don't believe it!" Plodnob said. "You convinced a Tyrannosaurus to become a vegetarian. Just like your ancestor!"

Stumbling away from the munching predators, Pointynog managed to compose himself and sort out what had happened.

Of course, it made sense, Pointynog reasoned. If he had been a Tyrannosaurus, and he had been faced with the option of deciding between food shelled in metal and chain that might find a way to fight back, or a meal wrapped in flimsy leaves that was already seasoned to taste, the choice would have been perfectly obvious!

Pointynog looked back to see Sir Jolley in motion at last. The ivory knight kicked over the crate of eels, and both Tyrannosaurus roared and headed straight for the fish.

As if in answer to that roar, the Tyrannosaurus that had been chasing Snicknik returned, the speedy knight now trailing behind him. All three ate happily, the breach of etiquette apparently forgotten.

"I did it!" Pointynog said. "I can't believe it."

"I can," Sir Jolley said. "I've always known."

Pointynog was startled. "You have?"

"Of course. Always remember, you're unique," Sir

Jolley said as he flicked a bug from his armor. "Just like everyone else."

Ironjaw glowered at Jolley. Then he turned to Pointynog. "You're a thinker, Pointynog. So think on this: The Troodon's body was wisely designed. We can neither pat our own backs nor kick ourselves too easily."

"I think that means we should go while our friends are having their meal," Pointynog said.

"Yes, indeedy, and while their meal isn't *us,*" Plodnob pointed out jovially.

Suddenly, the trio of Tyrannosaurus turned from their meal and approached the small group of knights and their lone human charge.

"They desire appeasement," Ironjaw said as he stepped away from the others. "You five must do what I did earlier. Only—you mustn't move. *Not one inch.*"

Beside Ironjaw, Nicholas was babbling. "It's been so long since I've had any real fun. I just wanted to have some fun, I meant no harm. . . ."

Pointynog opened his arms, holding his shield out to one side, his lance to the other. The other four knights mimicked his actions.

The Tyrannosaurus who had first approached Ironjaw broke from the other two and came to Pointynog. He roared and then lunged forward, snapping his jaws inches away from Pointynog's breastplate. Then he backed away.

The second rex bit at the air before Seeno's chest.

The third lunged at Snicknik.

Not one of the brave knights moved, though several trembled, and Plodnob nearly fell over backward.

Satisfied, the rexes went back to their meal.

And the caravan moved quickly away.

CHAPTER 9

Before nightfall, the caravan was met by two other groups of travelers, including one with a practically empty carriage. The five knights and Nicholas piled inside, and their journey continued.

"Pointynog, you look troubled," Nicholas said. "If it's about my actions, I assure you—"

"Not your actions. Ironjaw's," the young knight said. "He *knew* that we would be meeting these other travelers. But he never mentioned it."

"Oh," Nicholas said. He looked relieved. "And you're wondering what else he knows that you do not."

Pointynog fixed Nicholas with his gaze. "As a matter of fact, I am. About any number of subjects."

"There is much to be curious about," Nicholas said.

Including you, Pointynog thought. "It's interesting. What you've said puts me in mind of something I read once."

"And what's that?" Nicholas asked cheerfully.

"That there are certain types of reptiles who suffer from a particular failing," Pointynog said. "I can't recall if it was snakes or not, but let's say it was, for the sake of argument."

"All right," Nicholas said. His smile never wavered. "For the sake of argument, I can say practically anything."

"I'm sure," Pointynog said. "These snakes I was talking about. They can change their very shadings when they feel threatened. Really, they can do it at will, camouflaging themselves for any number of reasons."

"I suppose if you live in a dangerous place, like the Rainy Basin, a talent like that would come in handy."

Pointynog got comfortable. He was keenly aware of the attention his fellow knights were paying to the exchange between him and Nicholas. It made him feel as if he was playing chess with the dolphinback. Movements, bluffs, and strategies.

"There's a problem, though," Pointynog said. "A failing, as I said. These snakes can only transform themselves for a limited period of time. If you stay close to one of them long enough, the snake will always show its true colors."

Nicholas put his hands up in surrender. "Well, I suppose if your feelings over Ironjaw keeping things from you are so strong, you might be best served by simply coming right out and telling him. I can't think of anyone who would want someone else thinking of them the way they might a devious snake."

"Oh, no," Pointynog said. "I wasn't thinking of Ironjaw that way at all. As I said, things I've heard about, things I've read—they sometimes just come to mind. There isn't necessarily a reason for it."

"Well, I'm relieved," Nicholas said. "Ironjaw saved my life today. He protected me from my own foolishness. I would feel terrible if I knew that anyone thought so little of him."

Pointynog looked away. "As I said, of him? Not at all."

Nicholas laughed. "Then all is right with the world."

"So you say," Pointynog muttered. "So you say . . ."

That night, the group made camp near a sparkling waterfall. Seeno was asked to watch over Nicholas while he slept. No one wanted to see the young sleepwalker come to harm because of his unusual condition.

Both Seeno and Nicholas watched as one of the lumbering longnecks stood very still and closed her eyes.

"I'm feeling snoozy," she whispered. And moments later, she was lightly snoring.

The other sauropods, five in all, stood nearby. They formed a kind of star, their heads all pointing inward from five different directions. Each of them, in turn, also fell asleep.

The longnecks were so large that they couldn't lie down without injuring themselves, so like horses, they slept standing up.

Nicholas gazed at the longnecks for a while, then reclined upon his bedroll. He twisted and turned, but he could not get to sleep. Finally, he lifted himself onto his side and addressed Seeno.

"It's frustrating, isn't it?" Nicholas asked.

"Pardon?" Seeno asked.

"I'm just saying it must be frustrating," Nicholas said. "When you know all the answers, but nobody bothers to ask you the questions."

"I don't know what you mean," Seeno said.

Nicholas smiled. "I hope you don't mind a little friendly chat. Sometimes it helps me to clear my head and sleep more soundly."

"Of course," Seeno said.

"It's just that I have the feeling, with your always blending into backgrounds, very few people ask you for your opinion," Nicholas said. "Whereas I see you as the type who probably knows much more than someone like Pointynog, but doesn't feel the need to show off."

"Pointynog is very clever," Seeno said. "But . . ."

"Yes?" Nicholas asked cheerily.

"I do have another gift," Seeno said. "A talent in addition to my stealth."

"But your talent of stealth is what amazes me," Nicholas said. "I've read in the ancient scrolls that the first Seeno was so quiet and had such a light touch that he could tickle the nose of a sleeping sauropod without waking him. Have you heard that tale?"

"It's not a tale; it's true," Seeno said.

"Come now," Nicholas said. "Back in Doondaw-dle, I once slept in the presence of sauropods. I know all too well just how lightly these longnecks sleep. I'm telling you, it's a thing that just couldn't be done."

Seeno wanted to argue the point, but he didn't feel at all confident that he could convince Nicholas with words alone. The dolphinback had a very strong will.

"So what's this other gift you mentioned?" Nicholas asked after a long pause. "Besides your stealth?"

"I can detect flaws," Seeno said. "Flaws of any kind, in any thing. Or person."

"Really?" Nicholas said. "Well, no one's perfect. I mean to say, I know I have my flaws. That talent of yours must be quite a burden sometimes."

"It can be," Seeno admitted.

"But it's a good thing," Nicholas said. "Perhaps one day, that is what you'll be known for. After all, it was your *ancestor* who performed those great feats of admired stealth, not you."

Seeno felt injured by the words. "I didn't mean to say that I wasn't stealthy."

"Oh, of course not." Nicholas looked over to the

huge bellies of the sleeping sauropods. They rose and fell as the saurians slumbered. "I don't know about you, but I see opportunity before you. Now. Tonight."

"I don't understand," Seeno said.

"Wouldn't this be the perfect opportunity to see if you could, indeed, match the feat performed by your ancestor?"

Seeno laughed nervously. "What you're saying is simply to amuse me. You can't be serious."

"Why not?" Nicholas asked. "Or is boldness no longer a virtue of knighthood?"

The young knight narrowed his gaze. Nicholas had a point. Seeno knew he was shy by nature. And very cautious. But how far would he get as a knight if he did not learn to take action? To be bold?

"All right," Seeno said. "I'll try."

"Good," Nicholas said as he scampered to his feet. "Meet me in the clearing. I have something to attend to before you begin."

Seeno agreed.

The Troodon rose and looked around the camp. Everyone appeared to be asleep. Drawing a deep breath, Seeno walked toward the field of longnecks. He crept between their heavy bodies, his armor glinting in the pale moonlight.

He saw Nicholas arrive nearby. He waved at Seeno, then watched the knight expectantly.

Seeno crouched and drew a handful of tall grass from the earth. Then he chose a sauropod and noiselessly approached a large tree on the edge of the clearing.

Quietly, Seeno climbed. Carefully, he crawled along a thick branch that stretched out above one of the longnecks' heads.

Moving with the slightest breeze, Seeno adjusted his breath so that it rose and fell with that of the longneck. He moved close to the snout of the saurian and inched toward its fluttering nostrils. He lowered the soft stalks of grass gently, brushing them lightly, then more insistently upon the longneck's nose.

He watched the nostrils flare and saw the snout rise and twitch, clearly the victim of an annoying itch. Not sure what to do next, Seeno lightly scratched where he had tickled the sauropod. The longneck settled back, his slumber undisturbed.

Seeno couldn't believe it! He had done it! He had been stealthy enough to tickle the snout of a sleeping sauropod and not wake the sensitive saurian!

A whisper came from below him in the near dark. "If at first you do succeed, at least try to hide your astonishment."

Seeno looked down to see Nicholas on a branch far below. The dolphinback held a huge pair of brass cymbals in his hands. "From the musicians among one of the caravans that joined us today," he said.

"You wouldn't," Seeno said.

Nicholas grinned. He pulled the cymbals back, then he laughed as he smashed them together!

CHAPTER 10

KLLL-ANNNGGG!

Chaos erupted as the group of longnecks cried out and scrambled about. Seeno nearly fell from the tree, but he managed to hold on for dear life.

He tried to spot Nicholas in the mad confusion, but he couldn't see the lad. The towering forms of the startled sauropods crashed together and thrashed about. Their stumbling attempts to get away from one another caused them to swing their necks and stamp their limbs into the ground for balance without looking where they were going.

Smaller saurians and humans shouted with fear and ran in every direction to escape the chaos. Stone and earth shot skyward and thunder cracked the night with each footfall!

The dim light of the moon flickered wildly as the sauropods collided and blocked out the sky. Seeno made his way back to the ground and had to rely on his innate stealth to gauge just where he should run and jump to avoid being pounded into a crater by one of the wide tree trunk–like sauropod feet!

In the chaos, he heard smashing and the crackling of wood benches and other constructs from saddles being broken apart.

Debris rained down. Then one of the sauropods smashed into another, shattering not only the benches and crates attached to his harness, but pulverizing one of the carriages that had gotten between them! A wheel sailed high into the sky and tore through a tent as it landed, leading to more cries.

Then the darkness lifted as the sauropods closest to Seeno parted, and Nicholas was revealed. The boy was standing at the edge of it all, unafraid and laughing!

The chaos ended quickly as the longnecks finally calmed down. Seeno went to Nicholas.

"Why did you do that?" Seeno demanded.

Nicholas gave a wide, exaggerated yawn. He stretched broadly. "I'm sorry, what?"

"Some of the travelers could have been hurt!" Seeno said. "Look at the damage!"

Nicholas's eyes grew wide with surprise as he surveyed the debris-strewn clearing. "What's going on? I thought Dinotopians were more tidy than *this*."

The clanking of armor sounded, and Seeno turned to see Ironjaw striding forward.

"Explain this," Ironjaw said.

Seeno didn't know what to say. He looked at Nicholas, who appeared innocent and confused. The cymbals in his hands had mysteriously vanished.

Then Ironjaw noticed the tuft of long grass in Seeno's hand. And above, one of the sauropods was rubbing his still itching nose against the high branches of a tree.

Seeno knew that chivalry demanded he take the blame. After all, he had not been forced into this particular bit of mischief. His own weaknesses had once again led him astray.

Nicholas stepped forward before Seeno could speak.

"I'd say it was an accident," Nicholas said. "From the look of things. I couldn't say for sure. I remember that I was asleep, and the next thing I knew, I was here. Fortunately, Seeno saved me—"

"Here is what happened," Seeno cut in. "I was trying to show I could do what my ancestor did. Tickle the nose of a sleeping sauropod without waking him. And I did. Then his nose twitched, and I scratched it for him. And then—"

"There must have been an accident," Nicholas said. "Did you slip and startle them?"

Seeno shook his head. "I—"

"In life, there are no accidents," Ironjaw said. He narrowed his gaze as he regarded the young knight. "Seeno, if you have a thing to say, then say it. Otherwise, let us make our apologies and salvage what dignity we can from this incident. After I have this squared away, I will watch over Nicholas myself to make sure he does not sleepwalk again."

"But he—" Seeno began. Then he saw the shining innocence in Nicholas's face.

Had the lad been sleepwalking? Walking and talking but completely unaware?

Seeno supposed anything was possible. He turned to the great longnecks. "Claw-brothers, you have my apologies. I am entirely to blame. When I return to Halcyon, I will ask that I be given the Punishment of Shame."

The head of the closest sauropod dropped down. The dinosaur studied Seeno, then the lad beside him.

"You have miles to go in your journey?" the sauropod asked Seeno. He angled his head toward Nicholas. "With this one at your side?"

"I do," Seeno said.

"That is punishment enough for you," said the longneck with a pointed look for Ironjaw, "and reward aplenty for us."

The longnecks moved off to find another place to sleep. Ironjaw accompanied them, deciding finally to leave Seeno alone with Nicholas. *Punishment enough.*

The boy hung his head. "This is the way of things for me. Shunned for reasons I don't understand."

Seeno felt terrible. He wished there were something more that he could do for the lad.

But there wasn't.

* * *

At sunrise, a small work crew was assembled to repair the damage suffered by the various saddles and carriages during the mayhem. One of the caravans had to stay behind, but it would be well protected. The other two would keep moving.

For what he had done, Seeno suffered the angry glares and unkind words of strangers—and the confused looks of friends—all day and night.

The next morning, alone atop one of the slow-moving sauropods, Ironjaw wrote this upon a scroll:

> *Lord Botolf,*
>
> *I write to you with a heavy heart. The hope that Nicholas might show some sign of change in his behavior around knights who are his contemporaries has failed.*
>
> *I recall the day Nicholas came to our shores. He carried a single personal object in his jacket: A bound copy of the legendary tales of Arthur and the Knights of the Round Table.*
>
> *Though he has never spoken openly of this, and the book disappeared shortly after he arrived, one could certainly appreciate the possibility that our young explorers might inspire some show of chivalry and honor in Nicholas. Or, at least, genuine interest that was not rooted in sad and cruel pursuits.*

Everywhere he goes, he spreads mischief and misery, and at no point will he even admit to the ghosts of his past, the things that clearly haunt and drive him down his unfortunate path to what, I fear, will be a most unhappy conclusion.

I turn him over to Captain Broadback with the hope that perhaps Nicholas will find, upon the open sea, some sense of joy and self-worth that so many have tried to instill within him over the past year.

Strength and Honor,
Ironjaw the Mighty

The knight set down his quill and reviewed his letter. He allowed the ink to dry, then sadly rolled up the scroll and prepared it for the messenger he would meet at the dock.

CHAPTER 11

The caravan traveled for several more days without incident. When the triumphal arches of the great city of Sauropolis came into view, only Nicholas and the Troodons continued to the port. They journeyed by carriage, Ironjaw and Sir Jolley riding above, Nicholas and the explorers within.

They reached the bustling port the next morning. A dozen sailing ships were docked in the harbor, along with a pair of submersibles for examining the wrecks that lay far below.

Nicholas was intrigued. "Do the crews of the underwater machines go in search of scientific knowledge? Or treasure hunting?"

"Knowledge is a great treasure!" Plodnob said. "So it's true either way!"

Walking beside the group, Ironjaw patted the jovial knight on the back. "Well said."

Nicholas nodded, his smile thinner than usual, and looked away quickly. He didn't like to be upstaged. No, he did not. And he promised himself that Plodnob would regret it.

Sir Jolley approached a fisherman and asked about the *Unity*, the vessel that would take them to the Outer Island. The ivory-clad knight returned and nodded several times in silence before the group.

"Is that one the *Unity*?" Snicknik asked as he pointed at a ship with a blue-and-gold banner. His attention quickly went to the other vessels. "Or that one? Or maybe that one over there?"

Sir Jolley cleared his throat. "Unquestionably not. Unless it were. Then it would be a different story entirely. If it might be so."

"The fisherman wasn't sure?" Ironjaw asked.

"Unequivocally it may not be so," Sir Jolley said.

"I see," Ironjaw replied. "Well, in any case, I must be off. I'm sure you'll find your way."

The young knights crowded around to say their farewells to Ironjaw.

Soon, only Pointynog was left.

"I have to know," Pointynog said. "What is it you're not telling me?"

"About what?" Ironjaw asked.

"Nicholas," Pointynog said.

Ironjaw laughed. "How many seasons have you watched me play chess?"

"Four."

"And you still don't know my strategies? In particular, the one that was unavoidable in this instance?"

Pointynog considered. "Show, don't tell?"

"Your days of being taught are now behind you," Ironjaw said. "But you will be a student, just like all of us, for so long as you live. And some things must be seen to be believed, and experienced to be understood."

"Very well," Pointynog said. He would have preferred a more straightforward answer—but he knew this was all Ironjaw would tell him.

Ironjaw set his gauntleted hand on the young knight's shoulder. "May you never miss a sunset or a rainbow because you're looking down."

Pointynog looked confused. "But if I don't look down, how will I see where I'm going?"

"Look ahead," Ironjaw said. "It's what we all must do."

Nicholas approached. "Fair travel to you. Thank you again for coming to my aid—"

Ironjaw cut him off. "Your work is to discover your work. And then, with all your heart, to go about it."

The elder knight nodded and departed down the long boardwalk.

Nicholas looked to Pointynog. "What an odd thing to say. He almost seemed cross, for some reason, don't you think?"

"I think one should never attribute to malice what may have another cause," Pointynog said.

"You're not only clever," Nicholas said. "You're wise."

Wise enough to keep an eye on you, Pointynog thought. He didn't believe for a moment that poor Seeno had gone about that mischief with the sauropods the other night without some provocation.

Unfortunately, Seeno was shy, and unwilling to lay blame on anyone but himself. He had simply accepted the displeased looks of his fellow travelers as part of his punishment.

"Do you play chess?" Pointynog asked Nicholas. "It's my favorite game. Strategy. Bluffs. Misdirection."

"I prefer other forms of entertainment," Nicholas said.

"I bet you do," Pointynog said. "At some point, you'll have to let me know what they are."

"Oh, I'm sure you'll guess eventually," Nicholas said.

Pointynog shrugged, certain that he had guessed already.

Elsewhere, Snicknik raced around, asking humans and dinosaurs about the *Unity* and her crew. He returned with a round-bellied man with a scraggly white beard and bald head.

"You lookin' for Captain Broadback and his lot?" the man asked. "I'd check the Raptortail Inn. In fact, if you like, I'll even take you there and point them out to you!"

The knights assembled and followed the man past several warehouses and inns, until they came to a small, unassuming shack at the very end of the dock, near the water. A pair of young boys were fishing nearby.

Their guide held the heavy wooden door open for the group and ushered them inside. The warm, golden glow of lantern light greeted them as they entered a small taproom filled with rickety round tables and hearty laughter. Human and saurian sailors abounded, one more colorful than the last.

Soon, they were all assembled near a large round table. Captain Broadback stood and introduced himself. He was a red-bearded, barrel-chested man, with huge muscular arms that strained the fabric of his white silk shirt. His eyes were dark and sharply curious, yet friendly. His smile was heartening. He wore dark pantaloons and thigh-high boots. Two large golden rings dangled from his left ear.

Several saurians were seated with the captain, including a Dilophosaurus who bobbed his large dual crests as he said he was the ship's surgeon, Saltybones, and a pair of Hypsilophodons named Silvus and Sirus, the ship's cooks.

A young woman named Grace O'Connell stood and introduced herself. She had silver hair, though she looked no more than four and twenty, and she was short, barely five feet. Her blouse was white with gold trim, her leggings midnight blue. She was the first mate—and Captain Broadback's beloved.

"So you'll be traveling with us," Captain Broadback said to Sir Jolley.

The ivory knight nodded. "Indeed we shall."

"It's the first I've heard of it," the captain said. He settled back in his chair and placed his meaty hands over his belly.

"No one told you?" Sir Jolley said in alarm. "Most peculiarly odd and strikingly daft, a *blunderous erratum,* inaccuracy and oversight. I—"

"Joking," Hardshell said softly. "He's just joking, I think."

"That I am," the captain said. "You're all most welcome."

Sir Jolley stopped sputtering and sank back with relief.

"Fortunate are those who can laugh at themselves," Plodnob said. "For they shall never cease to be amused."

"And laughter is the shortest distance between two people," Grace said. "I think we're going to have a lovely voyage."

"I want to see the ship!" Nicholas said.

"I miss her, myself," the captain said.

"He only says that to make me jealous," Grace told the knights.

The group rose as one and headed for the door.

CHAPTER 12

The *Unity* was a beautiful ship and one of the most prized fishing vessels on Dinotopia.

The ship had the duck-shape design of a Chinese junk, with two masts and furled-up spare sails on the open deck. The tops of its masts were decorated with colorful paintings of humans, dinosaurs, and mythological creatures like gryphons, centaurs, and fairies. The polished wooden hull was beautifully trimmed in gold, blue, and maroon. And at the head of the bow was a splendid carving of a Giganotosaurus head with dark eyes peering out toward the open sea.

The crew was a dozen sailors. Huge fishing nets were tied off the bow.

Pointynog watched Nicholas as they boarded. The lad showed no sign of nervousness at all despite having fallen overboard on his last voyage. All that seemed to be forgotten the moment he was the center of attention.

The *Unity* set off hours later and was soon sailing along the Dragonfly Coast of Dinotopia. The entire island was ringed by dangerous reefs and there were unpredictable storms, making it impossible for outside ships to venture near and Dinotopian ships to venture outward. But safe navigation was possible around the island itself, as long as ships stayed within the channel between the island's shoreline and the surrounding reefs.

After they were under way, the captain gave the lads a tour of the ship, and Nicholas spoke up at every turn.

"I know why you wear those earrings," Nicholas said.

"And why's that?" responded the captain.

"It's an ancient belief that by piercing one ear, the sight is improved in the opposite eye," Nicholas said. "That's why the skipper pierces the ear on the opposite side of the eye used for a telescope, and why watchmen pierce both ears. It's to help them to keep an eye on everything around them. In the West Indies, one is worn only to help promote good health. And building workers in the States wear one after surviving a fall."

"Quite interesting indeed," the captain said happily. "And all quite true!"

Nicholas shrugged modestly. "Well, you know what they say: You may not know all the answers, but you probably won't be asked all the questions, either."

The captain laughed and clasped his meaty hand

on Nicholas's shoulder. "So you like sailing ships, do you?"

"I like anything that's new and different," Nicholas said. "New challenges. New mysteries."

"And new ways of having a bit of fun?" Pointynog asked pointedly.

"Exactly," Nicholas said. "Nothing bad ever came out of a bit of fun. That's how I see it."

Standing apart from the group, Sir Jolley grasped at the rail. He looked like he was going to be ill. Saltybones went to him, and led him away.

"He looks seasick," Nicholas said. "I've heard that can be fatal."

"Quite true," Captain Broadback said. "We'll have to keep the knight from sweets, and keep him to a diet of salt water and dried fish."

"We should also be sure there are no wags aboard," Pointynog said. "I've heard of pranks that are pulled on tenderfoots, like having someone who's seasick swallow a bit of meat on a string, then hauling it up. Or getting him to swallow a bumper of fish gurry."

"Well, now!" the captain said. "Two of you who know the ways of the sea!"

Pointynog nodded slowly to Nicholas. "It's always best to know the things that may go wrong, and to protect against them."

The captain smiled. "There are no wags on this ship, I assure you. And if there were, they would be swiftly dealt with."

The day went on, with the captain explaining the mysteries and fascinations of certain knots, of scrimshaw made from the bones of the deep dwellers, the marine reptiles that still prowled the ocean, and the special phrases the mariners used.

"One wrong turn of phrase can spell disaster on the sea," Captain Broadback explained. "The seas break against your ship, the wind roars in the rigging, the ship grunts and groans, a broken line flogs a sail, so many sounds, so many distractions. The captain or his mate on the poop or the bridge must be able to hear what the lookouts forward or at the masthead have to say.

"And when the weather is at its worst," continued the captain, "when the sailors are tired or sick or addled for whatever reason, my words must be understood. That's why the words we use are short, bold, and unlike one another. I could tell the helmsman to point the bow more toward the wind or away from the wind, but there is far less chance of confusion if I say 'come up' or 'fall off.' I might say 'luff' to bring the ship closer to the wind when we're about to be overpowered, or 'bear away' to leave the wind behind."

"But there are other reasons for using such phrases," Nicholas said.

"Yes," Pointynog intruded. "The mariner doesn't want the sea finding out about his business."

"Quite so!" the captain said. "Rather than say

you're 'going to sea,' you might say that you're 'going the whale's way.' An 'oar' becomes an 'ash.' A ship is a 'lone wanderer,' or a 'far flier.' "

The captain taught them about reading the weather, and again, Nicholas and Pointynog vied to prove who had the greater knowledge.

"Meteorologists refer to clouds as cumulus, cirrus, altocirrus, and such," Pointynog said. "But to the mariner, they are thunderheads, mares' tails, and mackerel skies!"

Nicholas raised his chin. "Mackerel skies and mares' tails make tall ships carry low sails!"

"If the clouds look as if scratched by a hen, get ready to reef your topsails then!" Pointynog retorted.

"If clouds are gathering thick and fast," answered Nicholas, "keep sharp look out for sail and mast. But if they slowly onward crawl, shoot your lines, nets, and trawl."

And so it went until nightfall. The contest between Pointynog and Nicholas was a draw.

This round, anyway.

After dinner, Nicholas yawned and turned in early.

Seeno approached Pointynog on deck.

"I'm worried about Nicholas," Seeno said from the shadows.

Pointynog jumped at the voice. "Good gracious, Seeno, give a knight some warning."

"My apologies," said Seeno. "But I have been thinking. My silence up to now came out of a sense of chivalry. But now that we are on a ship, my silence might endanger the very boy we have been asked to look after."

"What exactly are you talking about?" asked Pointynog.

"The other night, when Nicholas was sleepwalking, he said and did things that could have led to his own injury. I admit that the fault was mine. It shouldn't have mattered if he was asleep or awake; it was I who chose to match the feat of my ancestor—"

"Wait," Pointynog said. "He *said* things when he was sleepwalking? What kind of things?"

Seeno gave the entire story.

"So you see," Seeno said, "it is very difficult to tell when he's awake or asleep. Anyone watching over him could easily make the mistake that I did. And one can't be responsible for the things he says or does in his sleep, so—"

"He wasn't asleep," Pointynog said.

Seeno was startled. "What?"

"A sleepwalker is just that—someone who walks in their sleep," Pointynog said. "They may mumble a bit, but carrying on conversations, with eyes wide open, such as you've described . . . no. The boy simply wasn't asleep. Therefore, he was quite responsible."

Seeno's gaze narrowed. "I think I should watch over him again tonight."

"Do you expect him to sleepwalk?"

"I believe I do."

"Then I'll alert the others as to what to expect."

That evening, when all was quiet on the ship, Nicholas pulled down his bedcover.

"Seeno," he said. "I'm surprised to see you. I thought it might be one of your friends. More's the pity."

The young knight did not look his way.

"Don't tell me you're upset over what happened the other night?" Nicholas asked. "I rarely have a chance for true fun. That's all it was."

Another knight appeared. The jovial Plodnob. "How's the lad?"

"He sleeps soundly," Seeno said. "I had worries that we might need to weigh him down with bells and chimes and chains, but it's not yet come to that. If he moves, if he makes the slightest sound, I'll hear it."

"Well, good then," Plodnob said. "I return to the revelries. Fare you well!"

"And you," Seeno said.

Nicholas paused. "What was that?"

Seeno didn't answer. Nicholas leaped from his bunk. He rapped Seeno's helmet.

"Ignore *that*," Nicholas said. "I dare you."

Seeno yawned.

"You think you're clever, but you're just a fool," Nicholas said. "Play all you want at games like this. You can't best me."

Seeno rose and stood before the empty bunk. He pulled the blanket up as if Nicholas were still there.

"Rest well, lad," Seeno said to the empty bunk. "May your dreams be happy ones."

"Fool!" Nicholas roared. He left his small private cabin and found the other knights above deck. They sat about, looking at the stars.

Plodnob was laughing. "I dreamed a dream in which I was not the dreamer. Isn't that odd?"

"I dreamed the halls of Halcyon were directly ahead and that we sailed with hearty hearts and ill-strung harps," Pointynog said.

Snicknik's claws tapped against a table. "I dreamed I ran a race against me, myself, and I. None of us won! But I'll have to admit, it was joyous and fun!"

"I dreamed I could lift up the curtain of night and set down the weight of the world," Hardshell said.

"What do you think Nicholas is dreaming right now?" Pointynog asked.

"Certainly I hope his dreams are happier than those of Sir Jolley," Plodnob said. "He moans and quakes and shudders and shakes."

Nicholas circled the knights. "I would think that would make each of you glad. He's hardly been generous or kind in your lot."

"Has anyone volunteered to polish his armor?" Pointynog asked. "You know how upset it makes him if even a blemish appears on it."

"All right, you've had your fun," Nicholas said. "Now stop ignoring me."

Pointynog began to pace. "As to the mizzen

backstay clung, I saw three lights and loud I sung. The Lizard Lights I do design, I wait your pleasure to resign."

"My pleasure is at its wit's end," Nicholas said. He crossed in front of Pointynog, but the knight casually slipped away from him without ever appearing to notice he was there.

"To dream a dream is all life seems," Plodnob said. "To dream awake is what's at stake."

"I'm not enjoying this," Nicholas said. "Maybe you'll stop if you hear my idea. Now listen. About Sir Jolley. Imagine how he would feel if his pure white armor suffered some . . . misfortune."

The knights stared up at the starry sky.

"Come now," Nicholas said. "You can't honestly tell me the thought has never occurred to you. I've seen the way he treats all five of you. Shabby and ill deserved. A little well-earned turning of the tables never hurt anyone, that's what I say. And it's a thing we can do together. Some fun we can all have. A harmless little thing."

Pointynog tapped Hardshell's arm. "Do you know what mariners call themselves? Shellbacks. It's true."

"I see what you're doing," Nicholas said. "It isn't right. It isn't fair!"

Footsteps sounded behind Nicholas. It was Captain Broadback and Grace. Finally!

"Here, now!" the captain said. "What's this here row?"

"They're acting like this is all a dream or something," Nicholas said. "Trying to convince me that I'm asleep. But I'm walking about. It's all nonsense!"

The couple passed Nicholas as if they hadn't even seen him.

"We're having a discussion on the nature of dreams," Pointynog said.

"The sea has dreams," Captain Broadback said. "In fact, that reminds me of a tale . . ."

Infuriated, Nicholas began singing and shouting at the top of his lungs, but nothing he said or did made anyone pay the slightest bit of attention to him.

Finally, he sank against the rail, angered and defeated. Had he gone mad? Was he dreaming? Had he told the tale of his "walking in his sleep" so many times that it had somehow become true?

He looked up and saw Pointynog watching him. "What's wrong, Nicholas? I thought nothing bad ever came out of a bit of fun. That's what you said."

The knights and the mariners exploded with laughter. Nicholas stared at them in shock. They knew.

They knew everything.

Seeno suddenly rose into view. "There is a flaw," Seeno said. "In you. In the things you do."

"And here I thought I was perfect," Nicholas said.

"No," Seeno said. "You're not. Would you like to know the nature of your flaw?"

Nicholas glared at him.

"I thought not," Seeno said. He turned his back on the lad.

So did everyone else.

"I'll tell you the same thing I told those other louts," Nicholas roared. He hopped onto the slick rail, moving perfectly in time with the rolls and falls of the ship as it cut through the waves. "Nothing any of you says or does matters. I can do anything. Anything, you hear me? Any—"

There was a loud cry and a distant splash. The knights leaped to the rail.

Nicholas had fallen overboard!

CHAPTER 13

Nicholas was gasping for air, his limbs kicking wildly, panic overtaking him. He couldn't swim. In seconds he would disappear beneath the water, and they might never find him.

He looked for something to grab hold of, some piece of debris like the one he'd clung to until the dolphins had carried him to the island. But there was none.

On the deck above, Hardshell knew that the thing Strongarm had warned him about at the end of his final test was at hand. He had to focus on his duty as a knight. Nothing else mattered.

With a hearty warrior's cry, Hardshell ran and leaped over the side. The water slammed his armored form like a fist. He felt its weight start to drag him down, but he used every bit of his massive strength to fight that pull.

He swam to Nicholas, reaching him just as the lad went under. His hand fastened on the lad's shirt, his claws ripping it, then he hauled Nicholas up, keeping his head above water.

Hysterical, Nicholas flailed about, fighting blindly. It made Hardshell's task that much more difficult. And soon his body was tiring, his legs cramping.

Then he heard the splashes of his unarmored companions. Turning, he saw them in the water, swimming frantically in his direction.

Hardshell used his last bit of strength to hurl the dolphinback to the waiting claws of his companions. Then the surface closed over him and his world became a silent, blue, sparkling fist that reached into his throat and clogged his lungs.

He tried to swim, tried to fight, but the harder he tried, the quicker he sank, until the shimmering light of the moon caressing the surface of the water looked like a silver sword dangling high in the heavens.

Then even that light was gone, and the darkness and a dreamless sleep swallowed him whole.

Nicholas was hauled on board. Then Snicknik, the quickest of them all, dipped beneath the surface of the turbulent water. Seeno followed with two members of the *Unity*'s crew. All four emerged and dived down several times in a row. But they found nothing.

"He's gone," Pointynog said in shock. He stood on deck, staring into the murky water. "He's truly gone . . ."

"He's fallen as only the bravest may," Captain

Broadback said. "His life to save another."

Long minutes passed as the rescuers dived and came back up for air. Then, surfacing one final time, the rescuers in the water saw Captain Broadback gesturing furiously. "On board! On board! All of you, now!"

"We can't!" Seeno cried.

"Please!" Snicknik said. "Our friend needs us!"

"I won't lose all of you!" Captain Broadback said. "Look about you!"

The waves had grown choppier, and it was becoming difficult for any of them to tread water.

The sickly Sir Jolley appeared and leaned over the side. "Knights, I command you, return!"

With heavy hearts, the Troodons slipped into the harnesses dangling from above.

"Heave ho!" cried the winch operator as he began to haul the rescuers out of the water.

"Brace yourselves!" the captain yelled.

But there was no time. An impact from below rocked the ship and nearly capsized it.

"What was that?" Pointynog asked when the ship finally settled again. He couldn't bring himself to think of his lost friend; not now, when they were all still in so much danger.

"A leviathan of some kind," the captain replied. "A dweller of the deep. It may only be confused, but that's enough to make it dangerous."

All watched as a dark shape rose beneath the water

and burst through the surface, creating another wave that rocked their ship.

When it settled, Pointynog saw the long sleek back and the crocodilian snout of a blue and silver Liopleurodon bobbing nearby. The air-breathing marine reptile had four flippers, each a dozen feet long, and shaped like wings. The saurian's mouth was filled with sharp, crooked teeth. Its eyes were alert and wary. A familiar form lay gasping upon its back.

"Hardshell!" Pointynog yelled.

Nicholas spun at the sound of the knight's name. The lad's face lit up for just an instant—and then he looked about suddenly and forced his mask of practiced disregard back into place.

Captain Broadback shook his head. "Be wary, one and all. It may be a trap. We'll have to think this one through, weighing our options carefully and—eh?"

The captain stopped as a huge breastplate clanked to the deck. Pointynog was out of his armor and in the water before even the startled Snicknik could react.

"Wait!" Sir Jolley cried.

Snicknik and Seeno dived in after Pointynog, with Plodnob struggling with his boot, hopping on one foot toward the edge, and freeing himself seconds before slipping over the side to land with a hearty splash!

The quartet of Troodons swam under the gigantic predator's unmoving fins and were all startled as the

Liopleurodon shook itself and created a wave that struck them hard. They were driven back as a cry sounded from the beast's back.

"What? What? Whaaahhh!" Hardshell hollered. Then he was gently tipped into the water near his friends and the marine reptile moved off, dipping under the water with a grace that surprised all.

Plodnob swam to his friend Hardshell and hugged him in the water, threatening to cause them both to sink. Fortunately, Pointynog, Seeno, and Snicknik were able to haul them both to the ship. Hardshell's armor put a strain on the winch, but soon they had him back on board to the cheers of everyone gathered on deck.

Everyone except Nicholas, who was examining the rips in his brilliantly colored topshirt.

"You know this is going to take forever to repair," Nicholas said. "Really, you should be more careful with those claws of yours."

Pointynog was so relieved that his friend was all right that he managed to resist the urge to toss Nicholas back in the water.

But only barely.

CHAPTER 14

The next day, Captain Broadback cast his nets and set his crew out in their fishing boats. A strange blizzard of little white fish spiraled below, like a tornado beneath the water.

"No one really knows why they do that," the captain said. "It happens but once a year. Luck is with us!"

Everyone was kept busy, including Nicholas and the knights, who were taught even more about the ship's operations. The subject of Nicholas's "sleep-walking" was not mentioned again.

Pointynog was especially intrigued by the ship's compass, and the mechanism used to keep the sharp and sudden rises and falls of the ocean from disturbing it.

"It's all a matter of weights and counterweights," the captain said. "The compass is kept in its own space, set apart and untouched by all that goes on around it."

"Like Nicholas, you mean," Pointynog said with a low growl.

"None of that," Captain Broadback said. "Such comments are hardly becoming one who wears the armor of the Unrivaled."

Pointynog raised his snout. "I may be blunt. But that does not mean what I say is untrue."

The captain assigned Pointynog an especially difficult task for the rest of the morning—hauling, preparing, and delivering fish to the ship's great hold. The young knight was none too happy about it, but he performed the task well.

When evening fell, Pointynog was exhausted but satisfied that he had helped the *Unity* to fulfill its mission. He was especially happy to have spent the day with Hardshell, who traded stories with him of glories they would one day see together as knights.

The crew and passengers gathered on the deck to watch the sunset as they ate their evening feast. The knights and most of the crew stayed close to Hardshell, showering him with compliments and good cheer.

Nicholas sat with Captain Broadback apart from the others.

"Honestly, I don't understand any of this," Nicholas said. "They act as if Hardshell did something remarkable by coming back to them. Truth of the matter is that he was lucky and nothing more."

"I think you may be a little confused," Captain Broadback said. "Or maybe you're just missing the point. Their friend was almost lost. They cherish him and wish to be close to him. There's nothing more complicated about it than that."

The captain got up and joined the others.

"But . . . I was almost lost, too," Nicholas said.

No one was listening.

Captain Broadback rang a bell. He instantly captured everyone's attention.

"A matter's come to me that is most grave indeed," the captain said. "I discovered a bit of tampering with the ship's compass. Small stones were placed in the weight and counterweight compartments, throwing off the compass's readings. If this had not been caught, we might have sailed far off course."

Murmurs of surprise and alarm rose from the crew and passengers.

"Pointynog," the captain said. "I know you weren't pleased when I punished you for your words earlier today. But though you are the leader of your mission, I am the captain of this vessel. So long as we are on it, my word is law. You should be ashamed for what you've done."

"But—but, I *didn't*!" Pointynog said.

"Among the passengers, I explained the workings of the compass only to you," the captain said. "And no member of my crew would do such a thing."

Pointynog looked to his friends, but they were as astounded as he was.

"If you can provide me with some other logical explanation for how or why this tampering may have occurred, then tell it to me now," Captain Broadback said. "Otherwise, pay tribute to the steel and your crest and accept responsibility for this."

Pointynog looked to Nicholas. The lad had displayed just as much knowledge of the workings of a ship as he had. Yet the compass was something he hadn't known. And the captain could have been wrong about his crew. There were surly types aboard, but . . .

"I can't explain it," Pointynog said. "But if taking responsibility for this act is the only way I can preserve my honor and the honor of the Unrivaled, then I will do it gladly, whether it is just or not."

"Very well," Captain Broadback said. "You will swab these decks until they are spotless, and you will do it this very evening. If the sun rises tomorrow and you are not finished, you will have another chance after we bring in tomorrow's haul."

Pointynog nodded solemnly.

"And you will do it alone," the captain added. "No help from any member of the crew or any other passenger."

"I understand," Pointynog said.

The captain sighed. "Now, onto another matter. Nicholas?"

The lad looked up sharply. He covered his face with his hands. It appeared flushed.

"Yes?" he said, his voice cracking. Lowering his hands, he revealed a slight smile. "I'm sorry. But it is nice, for once, not to be blamed for anything and everything that goes on around me!"

"You are no more likely a culprit than any of Pointynog's friends," Captain Broadback said. "Unless there is something I don't know about?"

"No, not at all," Nicholas said.

The captain pointed to Hardshell. "Nicholas, have you nothing to say to him?"

"Well, one thing," Nicholas admitted grudgingly. "Why did you go in the water while wearing your armor? If you had thought it through, you would have known it would drag you down."

Pointynog rose to his feet and darted toward the ungrateful lad. Hardshell grabbed his friend and gently set him down.

"The deed was its own reward," Hardshell said. "We're both here to see the stars tonight. That's enough for me."

"Then you are unique in your generosity and deserving of my thanks," Nicholas said. "That, or not terribly clever!"

"I am a knight of the Unrivaled," Hardshell said. "I don't need or desire to be anything else."

Nicholas's smile faded. "I see. Then you are fortunate indeed. Most of us have wants. And many are cursed with the knowledge that what we want most will never be ours."

"All things are possible," Hardshell said. "And wants may change."

The group sat in silence. The only sounds were the low rush of the tide, the creaks and moans of the ship, and a *cawrrr* from a Skybax crossing high in the starry sky.

Nicholas excused himself and climbed into the rigging to watch the stars. He smiled and appeared carefree.

Captain Broadback watched him for a time. The captain looked as if he were waiting for something. Then his expression darkened. He shook his head and turned away.

Several hours later, Nicholas lay in his bunk, staring at the dark ceiling. He felt guilty.

It wasn't something he was used to feeling, or something he liked feeling. He wanted to shuffle the feeling off to whatever place he had exiled all such feelings in the past, whenever a twinge of such an emotion would come to him. But he couldn't. Pointynog had done nothing wrong.

Nicholas knew about ship's compasses from the last vessel he had been on. And he had heard Pointynog's remark about him earlier, so he fixed the compass while the captain was napping nearby. But no one knew any of that. He was totally in the clear.

Still . . . As difficult as it was for Nicholas to even contemplate, he was going to have to confront Captain Broadback and tell him the truth. This feeling, whatever its origin, was very strong, and would not go away otherwise. Nicholas was certain of it.

Nicholas slipped out of his bunk and made his way to the captain's quarters. The very gentle and kind Grace told Nicholas that the captain was visiting Sir Jolley. The Troodon's "stomach flu"—really, a severe case of seasickness—was finally starting to ease.

Nicholas passed Pointynog, giving the grousing Troodon a wide berth as he swabbed the deck, and went to the hold where Sir Jolley was resting and paused before his cabin door.

He could hear voices. So he resolved to wait until Captain Broadback and Sir Jolley had completed their chat. Confessing to *one* was a daunting enough proposition. The idea of unburdening himself before a pair was too much for him to bear.

He tried to find a comfortable place to sit, but there didn't seem to be any. Clutter was everywhere he looked, except the spot on the floor directly before the cabin door. With a sigh, he took his place there.

Then he heard what was being said within.

"So it is to be the Tribunal for the boy," Captain Broadback said. "I'd hoped it wouldn't come to this."

"Yes," Sir Jolley said. "Poor Nicholas."

Nicholas gasped. *The Tribunal? What is that?* he wondered. *It sounded terrible.*

"I had hoped it could be avoided," Captain Broadback said. "I thought it possible that he would come to appreciate the wonders of the sea, the pleasures we take in its mysteries, the joy we find in our work. But he is unaltered. Even Hardshell's sacrifice has not moved him."

In a weak voice, Sir Jolley responded. "Are you certain what happened today was *Nicholas*'s fault?"

"Yes," the captain said gravely. "He thought I was asleep when he performed his latest mischief with the ship's compass. But I was wide awake. I witnessed all."

Nicholas's eyes grew wide. The captain had been asleep. He'd been certain of it!

"And he allowed Pointynog to be punished?" Sir Jolley asked.

"He took pleasure in it," the captain said. "Even if he came to me now, unbidden, penitent, it would make no difference. He has much to learn, but I will not be his teacher."

"I've dealt with many difficult students," Sir Jolley said. "They can change. They can surprise you."

"That may be so," the captain said. "But I have made my decision."

"The Tribunal," Sir Jolley said. "It is rarely convened."

"He is a rare case. Though it pains me to say it, I honestly believe he will only learn when he must, when all other options are taken from him. It is unfortunate, but he has been extended every kindness, and you have seen how he has reacted to these efforts. Could you, in all good conscience, speak on his behalf?"

Nicholas listened, his heart thundering. He waited, but Sir Jolley did not reply.

Shaking, Nicholas crept from the door. So he was being taken to a "festival," was he? Well, there may well be a festival, but there was also a tribunal. The very word made him shudder.

He was to be called in front of some Dinotopian council to account for his acts. To stand by as others recited his wicked deeds and passed judgment on him. And what punishment might they mete out? Banishment to one of the small islands?

Or something worse?

He left the hold, and went about the only option he believed left to him.

Seeno woke instantly as Pointynog leaped down to their bunks. The first rays of the golden dawn filtered through a round portal, lighting up the clever knight's worried face.

"What's wrong?" Seeno asked as the others slowly woke.

"I've looked everywhere," Pointynog said. "One small boat is missing, and so is Nicholas."

CHAPTER 15

In their quarters, the knights put on their armor and gathered provisions for their journey.

"I don't want to wake Sir Jolley to tell him about this," Pointynog said. "This is our mission. We should find Nicholas and get him back to the ship ourselves."

"But Sir Jolley is our teacher," Plodnob said.

"He was," Pointynog noted. "He accompanies us now as our adviser. I do not see any call for seeking his advice."

"And Captain Broadback?" Snicknik asked.

"I'll speak with him," Seeno said.

The others turned in surprise to stare at the soft-spoken knight.

Seeno turned to Pointynog. "Please don't take offense, but he seems none too pleased with you at the moment."

"I can't argue with you there," Pointynog said. "Though I would argue with his reasons."

A sudden growl escaped Plodnob's belly. "We'll eat on the way?"

Pointynog laughed despite himself. "Yes, Plodnob. We'll eat on the way . . ."

Fifteen minutes later, the knights were in two boats that were being lowered over the side. Captain Broadback watched with a stern look. Grace stood beside him, concern in her deep brown eyes.

Seeno, Pointynog, and Plodnob took out the first boat. Hardshell and Snicknik followed.

They headed toward a vast sandy shore. The *Unity* had been anchored all evening. Pointynog had no idea how much of a lead Nicholas had on them, but he was certain this beach was the only place the lad could have made a landing. The beach was ringed by a dense jungle. There was no better place to make landfall for a dozen miles in either direction.

"The flaw has begun to appear," Seeno said as he rowed hard against the choppy water.

"What flaw?" Pointynog asked.

"Nicholas. The misery he brings to others is slight compared to the unhappiness he causes himself," Seeno said. "He tries to be a wretch. The simple truth is, he's no good at it. He has a conscience. It's been buried for a long time. But it's there, nevertheless."

"A cad with a conscience," Plodnob said. "I would call that a flaw. But a good one. One filled with promise, at the very least."

"If it's true," Pointynog said.

They closed on the shore and were surprised to see no sign of the boat Nicholas had taken.

"He couldn't have dragged it ashore and hidden it, could he?" Plodnob asked.

"I don't think he would have the strength," Seeno said. "Perhaps he put in further down the shore."

Pointynog shook his head.

"He may not have rowed to the mainland," Seeno said. "Perhaps he made for the breakers."

"I'm sure he would love for us to think that," Pointynog said.

"Why?" Plodnob asked.

"He wants us to waste precious time," Pointynog said. "That way we can be certain to fail in our first task as knights. That's what this is all about."

"You don't know that," Seeno said. "Try to keep an open mind."

"I am," Pointynog said.

Seeno's gaze narrowed. "No, Pointynog. You're not. You're seeing this as another competition and that isn't necessarily the way *he* sees it."

"Come on now," Pointynog said brusquely as he rowed even faster. "We can't make footprints in the sands of time sitting down."

The knights leaped from the boats and hauled them to the shore. Pointynog asked everyone to be still as he looked around at the sand, trying to spot Nicholas's trail.

"He could have set the boat adrift, then swum to shore," Pointynog said. "Or sunk it. Yes, that makes more sense."

"He's acting like he's playing chess again," Seeno said to Snicknik.

The speedy dinosaur nearly trembled with anticipation. He had been away from the far reaches of land for so long that he couldn't wait to race about!

"Chess, strategy, surveying the field, I quite agree," Snicknik said hurriedly. "And this time he doesn't want a stalemate!"

Pointynog began to pace. "I don't understand. Why are there no tracks? No trail to follow?"

"I'll go look!" Snicknik volunteered.

"No!" Pointynog said firmly. "You'll leave so many footprints with all your running around that we'll never find the ones Nicholas left behind."

He sighed and glanced over at Plodnob.

Plodnob laid a claw on his friend's shoulder. "Be of good cheer. The day is young, and success is assured if we but picture it and follow our dreams and imaginings. Remember, those who bring sunshine to the lives of others cannot keep it from themselves."

"Hmmm," Pointynog said. He turned and spied the highest, sunniest spot off the shoreline. It was a craggy overhang several hundred feet up among the rocks. "Maybe you're right!"

Twenty minutes later, Pointynog and the others stood upon the overhang, looking down upon the beach. The trail stopped near the boat; that much was clear to see. But something else was evident, something Pointynog may have never noticed without gaining some distance on the problem.

"Look there," Pointynog said. He pointed to a long straight stretch of sand with no hints of disturbance whatsoever. It blended into its surroundings up close, but from this distance, it looked unnatural, like a neatly kept carpet laid upon a messy floor. That the "carpet" and the "floor" were both made of sand created a certain illusion up close. But from here, it was clear that someone had covered his tracks as he departed.

"I see just where Nicholas went," Pointynog said.

The knights set out under the hot sun. Soon, the trail they followed through the jungle led them to a cave. They halted when they were within sight of the cave's entrance.

"I should go first," Seeno said. "If he hears the lot of us, he may run again."

"No," Pointynog said. "I'll go alone. If any of us has a chance of reasoning with this dolphinback, it's me."

"You?" Seeno said. "Are you sure this isn't just part of the game you believe you and he are playing?"

"Hard as it is to admit, I'm not sure of anything," Pointynog said. "I just have a feeling, that's all. One I can't logically explain."

"Good enough for me," Seeno said.

Pointynog drew a deep breath and continued up

the path to the cave entrance. He pushed aside the huge fronds masking the entrance and heard a short gasp from within.

He went inside as Nicholas stood to face him.

"So you've come to drag me back, have you?" Nicholas said. "I won't go."

"Fine," Pointynog said. "Do you mind if I sit awhile before returning to the ship? My feet hurt from all the time I've spent chasing my tail trying to make sure you were all right."

Nicholas looked away. Pointynog found a large boulder and used it as a resting couch.

"What did you think to accomplish?" Pointynog asked.

Nicholas looked away. "I didn't think."

"Well, perhaps that is the beginning of all your problems."

"You have no right to judge me. My affairs are my own."

"And so they would remain, if your actions didn't draw all of us into them."

"Is that why Hardshell was willing to give his life for mine?" Nicholas asked. He rose brightly. "Yes! Of course! That makes sense. He had his own selfish reasons. He didn't wish to face the shame of failing in his quest. Death before dishonor. I've read about such things!"

Pointynog sighed. "Tell me, could you also manage to convince yourself that if you built a big enough boat with a strong enough sail that you could venture off to the moon with a pair of cheese-eating rexes at your side?"

"That's absurd."

"So is what you're saying about Hardshell. He risked his life for yours. Not out of selfishness, but out of concern for you."

Nicholas hung his head, knowing in his heart that Pointynog was right. "Well, then he shouldn't have risked his life for mine after all," confessed Nicholas. "His was the more worthy."

Pointynog was stunned.

"Don't be so surprised," Nicholas said. "I know what I am, and I don't need a tribunal to tell me. That's why I fled. I won't be judged. And I won't be punished. I'll sentence *myself*. Right now. This day. I'll live alone here in this cave. I never asked to come to Dinotopia, you know. I had a destination in mind when I got on that ship. This place was not it."

"What are you babbling about?" Pointynog asked. "What's all this about a tribunal?"

Nicholas told Pointynog everything he had overheard between Captain Broadback and Sir Jolley— that his destination was not really a festival as they'd told him but some sort of terrible court of judgment.

"I'm nothing to you," Nicholas challenged, "except a means to an end. Deliver me to my fate, then take your leave, and you will have completed your first task as knights."

Pointynog shook his head. "It's true that we have been given a task, and that as knights, our honor is at risk if we do not complete it. But you are mistaken in your conclusions. There is no court of judgment and punishment. That is not the Dinotopian way. And as to how we feel about you, Nicholas—"

"—and why should I care about your honor anyway, Pointynog?" Nicholas cut in. "It's not like I have any of my own."

Pointynog studied Nicholas for a long moment. There had to be some way to persuade him to come back to the ship. Some way to change his heart.

Suddenly, Pointynog recalled the words of his fellow knights on the subject of Nicholas: *The misery he brings to others is slight compared to the unhappiness he causes himself. He tries to be a wretch. The simple truth is, he's no good at it. He has a conscience. It's been buried for a long time. But it's there, nevertheless . . . A cad with a conscience.*

"Let me ask you this then," Pointynog finally said. "Do you not at least feel that you owe Hardshell a debt for saving your life? Because *his* honor will also be lost if we fail to bring you to the festival. Not just mine."

Nicholas weighed these words in silence for a good long minute. Then he finally met Pointynog's eyes. "All right, I'll go with you. But not because I feel I owe anyone a debt. And not because I care one bit

112

about your honor or the honor of your dull-witted, strong-armed friend."

Though it was difficult, Pointynog ignored the insult to his friend. "Why, then?"

"I'll go with you for one simple reason: To prove to you that I am right and you are wrong. That there *is* a tribunal that will convene to judge me and mete out punishment. They you'll be forced to see the truth about your Dinotopian world," Nicholas said. "You believe your society to be so different from that of the outside world? I want to see your face when you realize that it's not. The Tribunal of Judgment will prove it."

"I say again," Pointynog insisted firmly. "There is no such thing."

"What do you know anyway? You didn't even know the proper etiquette for meeting a Tyrannosaurus in the Rainy Basin!" Nicholas hollered. His voice echoed in the close confines.

"What kind of life did you come from in the world outside that you could even imagine such a thing as a Tribunal of Judgment?" Pointynog asked.

"Why do you care to know?" Nicholas asked.

Pointynog shrugged. "Why do you care to keep it secret? Are you ashamed?"

Nicholas laughed. "Hardly. I come from wealth and privilege."

"That much I had guessed."

"You don't understand. My father was poor to start with, but he had a keen mind, and while working in factories, he saw inefficiency and became inspired to invent things that would make production simpler, quicker, and somewhat less dangerous. It made him a rich man."

"Is it that you miss your family? Do you stay awake at night, wishing you could tell them you were safe and—"

"I have no loved ones," Nicholas said. "Not any more."

Pointynog waited.

"My mother died during my birth. When I was eight, my father enrolled me in a private school not far from our home. I could see him every weekend, and I did. Such a thing was rare at Collingsworth, the school I attended. Most parents only saw their children on holidays. I knew my father was a good man. He shared with me his hopes and dreams for the future, and he asked that I do the same with him. He was my best friend.

"Then one night, the news came. My father died in an accident at one of his factories. I was in my room at Collingsworth, alone and shattered, when a knock came at the door. It was a lad named Joshua.

"I was shocked to see this boy. Joshua had made his disdain for me clear from the day I arrived at the school. He had said flat out that I was a lesser thing because he and his friends were the children of gentle people born to wealth, and my father was a commoner who had gotten lucky when he shouldn't have.

"It was due to Joshua that I had no friends at Collingsworth. He made certain I was shunned from my very first week at the school. I had never told my father because I did not want him to think less of me. So I carried on, hoping that one day Joshua and the others would see that I was worthy of being included. That I *did* belong there.

"When Joshua and his friends came to me that night, it filled my heart to bursting. They took me into their circle. They called me friend. I thought *finally* I belonged. That I was accepted.

"And then, after a year, I saw the letter. It was meant for another student, a member of Joshua's circle with a name similar to mine. But it had been mistakenly delivered to me. Joshua had been on a holiday with his family and wrote to him at Collingsworth, revealing at last the true depths of his hatred of me. His friendship and the others' had been an elaborate pretense. It had all been a ruse, a mask.

"I had trusted them as friends. I believed all they told me. Yet even on the night my father died, they had been conspiring. The group had met secretly to decide how to befriend and use me.

"You see, upon my father's death, I became the sole heir to a very great fortune and the head of my father's factories. Those factories used wool and grain and other resources in the surrounding farmlands to create textiles and other things.

"Joshua and many of his friends were from families who had high and mighty names and estates. But those estates had dwindling incomes. They needed exclusive contracts with my father's factories to bring wealth back to their names. They needed higher pay for their farm goods, too. And after they befriended me, I saw to it that they got everything they asked for.

"Then I saw the letter, and I nearly ran to Joshua, to confront him, to vent my rage upon him.

"Instead, a coldness came into my heart. And a hard determination. I tossed the letter in the fire and acted as if it had never come my way. For the entire year after that, I slowly turned the tables on those boys, though they had no awareness of it happening.

"This time *I* was the one who acted the part of the 'friend.' I was the one who perfected the art of wearing the mask. And behind their backs, I began a chain of events that would ruin their families completely.

"I vowed to never again be tricked by a false friendship or a selfish interest posing as an offer of kindness. My eyes were finally opened, and I would use my new vision to see through everything and everyone. I grew stronger and stronger, and I saw just how weak and stupid Joshua and his friends were.

"You see, what I learned was how to make my own rules to live by. Unfortunately for me, those rules didn't work as well outside the little circle I controlled.

"When I ventured on a voyage with my lawyers and accountants to meet with an importer from another land, which would make my father's factories even richer and more powerful, I fell overboard. I had not really been sleepwalking, you see. I had gone onto the deck at night and tripped over a bucket. I insulted the sailor who'd left it there. Then he insulted me, claiming I couldn't walk straight on land, let alone a ship. To prove him wrong, I climbed onto the rail and balanced myself on it."

"And you fell overboard," said Pointynog.

"Yes," said Nicholas, his head lowering. "I was stupid and arrogant. And now I've lost everything. And that sailor was no different from Joshua and his band. He called no alarm. Just laughed at me from the rail, pleased to let me drown as the ship sailed on into the night."

"So that's your whole story then?" Pointynog asked. "I suppose it's as good as any."

"You say 'story' as though it's not true," said Nicholas bitterly. "But it is true. I swear to you."

"I don't doubt it," Pointynog said. "I'm simply not moved."

"You don't understand," Nicholas cried. "What they did to me, what I felt—"

Pointynog yawned. "Sorry. You weren't done yet?"

Nicholas's face flushed. "I should have known better. I've shared something with you that I swore I would tell no one else, ever, and this is how you react?"

"We've all had wrongs done to us," Pointynog said. "Whether it be by random circumstance or deliberate action, life is seldom fair. We cannot control the things that come our way. But we can control how we *react* to them. Everyone makes choices, Nicholas. You have chosen not to trust anyone on Dinotopia who extends you a hand or claw. You condemn all in your present because of your treatment by a few in your past. But you are not justified in this simply because of what you endured. Show me, instead, the face you showed your father. Return to the open heart you once had as a child."

"Impossible."

"Can you not recall the hopes and dreams you once had? The ones you shared with him? Can you not recall the innocent things that brought you true joy? Do that, and the world will change before your very eyes."

"So you say."

"Yes. And I always say exactly what I mean."

"Take me back," Nicholas said. "I have nothing more to tell you."

"That's a pity," Pointynog said.

"I'm sure you'll get over it."

"No," Pointynog said. "It's a pity for you."

CHAPTER 16

Nicholas was quiet and sullen as the *Unity* rounded Cape Turtletail and traveled northeast along the eastern coast of Dinotopia. The great green stretches of the lower peninsula gave way after a stop to fill the rest of their holds with fish at Silver Bay, turning to the hard, dry lands of the Great Desert.

It wasn't until they passed the port of Neoknossos, north of Chandara, that he spoke at all, and even then, he seemed to be mumbling to himself.

"A bit further inland and we might visit the Tomb of Mujo Doon," Nicholas said. "The chance is gone now, like everything else . . ."

Though he spoke to no one in particular, his words were heard by one of the Troodon knights. Sir Jolley approached Grace, one hand on his now only slightly upset stomach, and told her about Nicholas's musings.

"You think there's something to be done?" Grace asked.

"Some people grin and bear it," Sir Jolley said. "Others smile and change it."

Grace went to Nicholas, several cords of brightly colored rope in her hand. "You know a thing or two about mariner's knots, don't you? At least from books. Would you like to feel some rope in your hands? There's much to learn."

"I . . ." Nicholas shrugged. "I suppose it might be a painless way to pass the time."

Grace only smiled, and began to tutor the lad.

As the *Unity* cut through the sunlit waves, Pointynog approached Sir Jolley.

"How are you?" Pointynog asked.

"I am better than I was," Sir Jolley said. "But not quite so good as I was before I got worse."

A short burst of laughter drew their attention. The knights looked over to Nicholas and Grace. The lad had formed a complex knot and seemed genuinely excited about it.

"That's an encouraging sign," Sir Jolley said.

Pointynog nodded slowly. There was so much he wanted to say to Sir Jolley. So many questions that he had after his conversation with Nicholas. But although he had not been sworn to secrecy, Pointynog felt a duty to keep all of what had passed between Nicholas and himself private.

"Encouraging," Pointynog said. "I suppose. Yet when I look at him, it's hard to see anything but shadows."

"Never fear shadows," Sir Jolley said. "That simply means there's a light nearby."

Across from the knights, Nicholas concentrated on the knots. He put on a bold display of slowly lowering the defensive wall that had surrounded him since his return from the mainland. The warm smiles and the encouraging words he elicited from Grace told him that it was all right to do so. He was safe.

It was all an act.

As Nicholas's hands moved over the ropes and complex patterns of brilliant color appeared, his mind stayed firmly fixed on his objective. Nicholas had been quiet for days because he had been observing his opponent. He had to know whether Pointynog had told anyone about the truths he had foolishly shared when they were alone. Now Nicholas was certain that Pointynog had kept the information to himself—and he could guess why.

Images formed in Nicholas's mind. He saw Pointynog speaking before the Tribunal of Judgment, revealing the secrets he knew about Nicholas at the most dramatic moment possible. Then Nicholas imagined the jealous looks of Pointynog's fellow knights as Pointynog won praise from those who had convened to pass judgment.

The knight's strategy would be his undoing. Nicholas knew how to work this to his advantage. He had rehearsed the exchange in his thoughts a hundred times:

"I'd like a word with you, Pointynog."

"About what?"

"You're going to forget everything I told you when we were alone. You won't say a word before the Tribunal."

"Why would I refrain? By telling the truth not only will I gain the satisfaction of seeing you humiliated, I'll win favor from my elders!"

"Because I can tell your friends that you revealed their darkest secrets to me."

"Nicholas, I said no such things!"

"True. But they won't know that I'm lying. It will make them lose faith in you. Your control over them, your trust, it will be gone. All with a few words from me. Now . . . can I count on your silence?"

"Yes, blast it. You can."

A sudden nudge from the fair silver-haired Grace made Nicholas start. "You looked deep in thought."

"I was for a moment," Nicholas admitted. "Happy thoughts."

She grinned and nodded at his hands.

He had been paying so little attention to what he was doing that he accidentally slipped the ropes around his own arms—and literally tied himself in knots!

The *Unity* moved off from the coast of Dinotopia and passed into the twenty-mile-wide chasm between the mainland and the Outer Island. Soon there was no hint of land in any direction. They might as well have been on the open sea.

Snicknik raced about, busily asking one mariner after another how much longer it would be before they reached the Outer Island.

"It'll take as long as it takes," Captain Broadback said when it was his turn.

"Everyone says that!" Snicknik said. Then he raced on to another sailor.

He asked the same question—and got the same answer. Snicknik doubled back to the captain.

"Isn't there anything we can do to get there quicker?" Snicknik asked. "I hear there are tiny winding streets with many obstacles scattered upon them where we are going, and I thought, there I could run, it'd be so much fun!"

"There are no shortcuts on the open sea," Captain Broadback said with a laugh. "And what fun would there be for us if there were? The journey's the thing. Not the destination."

Snicknik ran off and raced around. And then he got bored with racing.

He spotted the spare sails. They were tied with so many tight ropes. If one of them needed to be used, it would take forever to get it free.

To be helpful, Snicknik flicked his claws at the ropes, fraying them one by one. Within minutes, he was done. *Now* if the captain needed the spare sails, they would be his with the slightest tug!

He turned, his tail catching on one of the frayed ropes. With a low growl he yanked it loose and ran off, careful not to collide with any of the mariners prowling the deck.

Suddenly, he heard a fluttering. A roar.

For some reason, he didn't like the sound of that. He stopped, and a massive shadow fell upon him. It looked like a curtain of darkness rising up to cover the sun. Turning, Snicknik saw the closest of the spare sails rolling and uncurling itself upon the deck! It rose up like a magic carpet out of legend. Catching the wind, the mammoth sail swept a dozen crewmen from their feet as it flew fully unfurled at Snicknik!

With a cry of alarm, Snicknik ran ahead, shouting for everyone to get out of the way!

The top of the sail was speared on a mast. The bottom whipped out and slapped Snicknik on the backside. The blow made him yelp—and sent him skidding toward the rail. Snicknik smelled the salt of the open sea and slid toward the brink!

Then a pair of gauntleted hands were on him, anchoring him in place.

Opening his eyes, he saw Hardshell crouching over him.

"There's another," Snicknik said. "Another, another, another—"

"Another what?" Hardshell asked.

Then the whipping sounds and the frantic shouts sounded again. Snicknik winced as he heard the fluttering, saw the shadows, and heard the tearing of the second sail he had freed.

"You didn't," Hardshell said.

"I didn't think," Snicknik said. He lowered his snout. "I never do."

It took half an hour, but the mess was quickly sorted out. Both of the backup sails had been shredded. The ship's master craftsman surveyed them sadly and said there was little he could do until they put in at their next harbor.

Captain Broadback was not pleased. He looked at Nicholas and said, "I'd like to know who was responsible for this."

Nicholas's shoulders sank and he looked away.

"It was I, it was me, it was myself!" Snicknik said as he raced forward. Breathless, he explained what he had done—and why.

"Indeed," the captain said. He looked at the frayed ropes, then at Snicknik's rapidly clicking claws. Clearing his throat, he looked back to Nicholas with a look of apology.

The lad was looking down and tying more knots. His face was set. Sitting beside him, Grace patted his back.

He shrugged off her hand.

"Snicknik!" the captain bellowed. "Do you understand that what you did was wrong?"

"I do, indeed," Snicknik said quickly.

"And is there any punishment I might mete out that would even begin to teach you the hard lesson that some things are done a certain way for a reason, and that speed is not always the most important factor in a process?"

Snicknik considered for all of a second, a lifetime for him, and shook his head. "No, probably not, unfortunately, I doubt it, I'd be willing to try, but it always ends with a sigh."

The captain did sigh. "You'll be punished anyway. For the duration of this trip, you are to sit *still*."

"I'll bind him for you if you want," Nicholas said without looking up.

Grace shushed the lad.

"It would be no bother," Nicholas said.

The captain looked to Pointynog and the other knights. "Can I trust you lot to watch him and make sure he endures the punishment?"

Pointynog was about to agree—but Snicknik was on his feet.

"Snicknik!" called Pointynog in alarm.

"There, there, I see it, there!" Snicknik called as he pointed toward the distance.

"It's too early for landfall," the captain said. Then he turned, along with every hand on deck. He gasped as he saw what Snicknik had spotted: A curtain of darkness was falling over the horizon. Jagged bolts of searing white lightning flared in its depths. Two huge swirling masses fought one another at its heart.

The wind shifted suddenly, with massive gusts punching at their sails and driving the *Unity* back. The ship lurched and rolled in the water, with practically everything that wasn't tied down skidding one way, then another.

On the deck, Sir Jolley grasped at his stomach as Pointynog and Hardshell took the elder knight below. When they returned, the sea had grown rougher.

Captain Broadback approached Pointynog as Hardshell went off to find the other knights.

"We've faced heavy weather before," the captain said. "There is always a risk. A storm may worsen. Things unforeseen may arise. And we are without benefit of additional sails."

He gestured to Grace, who brought Nicholas forward.

"We have no business in the Outer Island other than delivering you lot to the Serpentine Cathedral," Captain Broadback said. "I'm willing to go on despite the danger, and my crew will follow wherever I lead. But the decision isn't up to me."

Pointynog eyed the captain warily.

"You must decide, young knight," the captain said. "Do we dare the storm or turn back? The responsibility for the consequences of either decision rests entirely with you."

CHAPTER 17

Nicholas watched the captain and Pointynog carefully. He could already feel the air growing damp and see the light around them beginning to fade.

"We swore an oath," Pointynog said. "On our honor as knights. If we fail in this, it will mean disgrace to all our houses. We will be shamed."

"I respect your wishes," the captain said as he turned and swiftly walked into the strong winds. "We press onward."

Nicholas felt his entire body tighten. *I knew it!* he thought. All this time, the knights cared nothing for him. His deliverance was a means to an end for them.

"Wait!" Pointynog said.

The captain hesitated. Nicholas inhaled sharply. The knots he'd been creating bunched in his hand.

"Turn back," Pointynog said firmly.

The captain glanced over his shoulder. The wind ripped at his shirt. "Are you certain? Despite what it may cost you?"

"What it will cost *me,* yes," Pointynog said. "I can only hope that as the decision rests entirely with me, that my friends will not share in what I'll face."

The captain nodded thoughtfully. "Very well. Grace, come with me."

Grace gave Nicholas's shoulder a gentle squeeze, then moved off quickly with the captain.

Pointynog looked to Nicholas. "I'm sorry."

Nicholas had been prepared for anything but this. His mind worked quickly, attempting to find a selfish rationale for Pointynog's actions, some gain that would counter the loss he was surely facing.

But he couldn't. None of this made sense to him. And now Pointynog was *apologizing*?

Nicholas looked at the young knight in confusion. Pointynog took a step forward.

"I said nothing of our conversation," he told Nicholas as he drew a thin folded-up scroll from his gauntlet. "But when we took Sir Jolley back to his quarters, he gave me this. Fearing the coming storm, and not knowing who would survive, he felt it was important that I know all. I read it before returning here."

Pointynog handed the scroll to Nicholas, then stood back as the lad opened it. Nicholas read the florid script several times. He could hardly bring himself to believe what he was seeing.

It read:

AN INVITATION

The Tribunal of Understanding petitions
the appearance of Nicholas Cross
at the below mentioned time and place.
The Tribunal is comprised of the
wisest and most open hearts
and souls alive on Dinotopia.
The presence of young Master Cross
is requested because it is felt he is unique.
All agree that he possesses a talent
that may prove a tremendous benefit
not only to himself,
but also to any he encounters.
The Tribunal wishes to ask young Master Cross
if he would agree to join with us
and share his gift.

Several names Nicholas had heard whispered with the greatest of reverence were listed below.

"It was to be given to you at the festival," Pointynog said. "The choice, Nicholas, was always meant to be yours."

Nicholas shook his head. "This is . . . this is a lie. It can't be real. Not after everything I've done. And— this gift they mention. I have no gift."

"You do," Pointynog said. "You only have to recognize it and direct it in ways you've never thought to before."

"But . . . why wasn't all this made clear to us before?" Nicholas pleaded. "Why—"

A sudden crash sounded from below and the ship tipped starboard. The invitation flew from Nicholas's hand, and he lunged for it but missed.

"No!" Nicholas cried.

Pointynog leaped high and snatched it from the air. He landed hard and skidded toward the rail.

Nicholas, holding firm to a net, reached out and grasped the Troodon's arm.

The ship slowly righted itself. Then another thunderous sound came and a shuddering impact rocked the ship again.

High above, the mainmast shuddered. When a third and final impact shook the ship, the mast shattered and collapsed, bringing the mainsail down with it.

The sail and several others caught by the collapsing structure were shredded as the mast smashed onto the deck with the sound of a giant's fist striking out in anger. Mariners were scattered as the wildly whipping fabric of the fallen sail cloaked much of the deck in darkness and confusion. Pointynog saw his friends racing his way, along with Captain Broadback and Grace.

The captain barked orders. Repair crews were on the scene quickly, cutting the fluttering sails loose and gathering what could be salvaged.

On the horizon, the storm grew closer. The waves rose and tossed the ship, and gigantic dark forms burst from the water surrounding the *Unity*.

A half-dozen Liopleurodons roared fiercely above the thunder and wind of the approaching storm.

"They must have smelled the fish in our hold," Captain Broadback said. "That's why we were rammed. They're hungry!"

"With our sails damaged, we have no chance of outrunning the storm," Seeno said. "We've failed."

"If things go wrong, don't go with them," Pointynog said quietly.

"What?" Snicknik asked.

The clever knight nodded in the direction of the Liopleurodons, who glided through the waves around them.

"Don't be so sure we've failed," Pointynog said. "I have an idea."

Suddenly, Captain Broadback called to them. "The six of you should be belowdecks. There are no ruptures. The *Unity* is built strong, and the fish in our hold have given us ballast. But it'll be rough going on deck once that storm approaches. And if anyone falls overboard this time . . ."

The Liopleurodon roared again. One opened its mouth, revealing its sharp, jagged teeth.

"The sea and its hungers," the captain said coldly. Someone called to him, and he turned away.

"We can't go below," Pointynog said. "We're

Knights of the Unrivaled. This is our place."

"Then I should go," Nicholas said. "It's not cowardice, but I have no business staying behind—"

"What if I said you did?" Pointynog asked.

More cries of alarm drifted to them beyond the buffeting wind.

"Grace! It's Grace!" someone yelled.

All thoughts of flight left Nicholas with those words. The knights followed him across the deck.

Grace was pinned beneath the fallen mast. Water was splashing on board the deck. Some of the crew were struggling to keep her head above water while others tied ropes around the heavy trunk of the shattered mast to move it.

"There's a flaw," Seeno said. "They cannot move it in time to save her."

The ship pitched as one of the Liopleurodons leaped from the water and fastened its jaws upon the railing. The behemoth's weight nearly capsized the ship and sent many sailors skidding toward the brink!

Nicholas's gaze met that of the great marine reptile. For an instant, the world melted away and he understood the creature's hunger and frustration. He had known an even darker hunger, one that had consumed him for years—the hunger for revenge.

When he had come to this island and learned he would never leave, he understood that his hunger would go unsatisfied for the rest of his days. His frustration and his distrust of anyone who would pose as a friend had caused him to lash out at every innocent soul he encountered.

"Let-it-go," Nicholas snarled at the Liopleurodon as he lunged toward the beast and the churning waters beyond. He snatched up a chunk of splintered wood and slapped the side of the Liopleurodon's long snout, which rose above them, dripping water and ichor upon them.

"You'll get what you want," he hollered, his side flush against the rail, the water only a few feet away. He struck the creature again. "Let go!"

With a cry that created a gust strong enough to blow back Nicholas's matted hair, the Liopleurodon released the ship. The *Unity* seesawed in the water, one side rising sharply, then falling, sending the crew and its passengers flailing wildly. Miraculously, none went overboard.

Nicholas and the knights went back to Grace. She was barely conscious. Her head had been struck several times as the mast pinning her had moved about, slamming her into platforms and railings. Water pooled around her head.

The mariners were back with their ropes, but all they could do was haul the mast and Grace.

"She's drowning—and it's crushing her!" the captain said in terror he could not disguise. This was his beloved. He could lose a thousand ships and replace them all. But the love they shared was a gift that was unique and could never come again.

"Nicholas, we need you now. Your gift is all that might save us," Pointynog said.

"I have no gift!" Nicholas called over the wind.

"You do," Pointynog said. "You've been using it all along, only not in a way that helped anyone."

"What are you on about? I don't understand!"

"Yes, you do! That's just it, Nicholas. You have the gift of understanding. You can see inside a soul and understand whatever it is you want to understand. Until now, all you've wanted to know is where someone's vulnerable, and how to hurt them with that knowledge. It's not the only way."

Nicholas watched Grace. He heard the captain moaning. For the first time in longer than he could remember, the sound of someone else's pain brought Nicholas no pleasure.

He looked to Hardshell. "Lift it."

"It might as well be as heavy as a Diplodocus hatchling! I'm not my ancestor. I—"

Nicholas looked into the young knight and saw all the strength that was needed.

"Lift it," Nicholas commanded. "Focus on that and nothing else. Just lift it."

The knight turned to the mast and pushed his way through the crowd gathered to help Grace. He bent low and angled his arms beneath the polished wood column. He felt hands on him. The strength of others anchoring him, keeping him from sliding on the slippery deck. And somehow, he felt their strength flowing into him.

The world fell away. He no longer heard the screams and wails of the storm. The images of chaos and confusion surrounding him vanished.

The world was silent and still. He had but one thing to do.

He lifted. Focusing every iota of his will, he used his strength and felt his muscles burn, ache, and strain. His back felt as if it could not stand the effort.

These distractions faded, too.

Lift.

And so he did. He heard a creaking, gasps, then someone saying, "Let it down, let it down!"

Hardshell came back to himself. He saw that Grace was in Captain Broadback's arms.

Pointynog was beside him. "Hardshell, let it down!"

Hardshell suddenly felt the pain in his rippling muscles. He looked down and saw that he had lifted the mast only a few inches, but that had been enough to slide Grace out from under.

He dropped the mast and stumbled back.

Lightning streaked across the sky and thunder shook the *Unity*. All around, the great marine reptiles roared.

"Captain Broadback, the hold!" Nicholas said. "Empty the hold, bring as much fish as your crew can carry to feed the Liopleurodons!"

"Foolishness," the captain said.

"No!" Pointynog said. He explained what Nicholas had done. How he had helped Hardshell to save Grace.

"It's the only way to get them to help us," Nicholas said. He looked to the steadily approaching curtain of darkness. "And we need their help."

Soon, the entire crew was in motion. Nicholas and the knights helped the captain and his finest craftsman take their wide nets and turn them into harnesses. Meanwhile, much of the hold was drained, and the fish they had caught spilled overboard to the ravenous marine reptiles.

"How do you know they won't just feed and move on?" Captain Broadback asked.

Nicholas shook his head. "I don't. All I can tell you is we have an understanding. We'll have to see if they keep it."

They did.

The well-fed Liopleurodons assembled on the port side of the ship and submitted as the harnesses were hung over their huge snouts. The storm was almost upon them.

"So many things can go wrong," Seeno said. "The lines anchoring the *Unity* to the Liopleurodons might come undone, the moorings might break, the ship—"

Pointynog put his claw on his friend's shoulder. "Not every *potential* flaw comes to fruition."

Seeno's face lit up. "That's true, isn't it!"

"Let's dwell on the things that may go right, not wrong."

Nicholas stood nearby, surveying the mass of sleek forms harnessed to the damaged ship. "There's something missing. Not a flaw. Just something I haven't seen."

Beside him, Snicknik raced and skidded to a stop. "Sorry. My punishment. Forgot for a second. My feet move faster than my thoughts. A problem I don't think I'll ever solve, though I try. I do."

Nicholas nodded. He stared at the speedy knight—and knew at once what was needed.

"Snicknik has to take the reins," Nicholas said. He pointed to the center Liopleurodon. "Out there. On the back of the beast."

Plodnob shook his head. "Are you joking? He'd have to be standing still."

Snicknik tapped his claws frantically. "Still? Standing still?"

"It should be me," Pointynog said. "This is my responsibility."

Hardshell stepped forward. "Let me do it. It's a ride I've taken before. True, I was unconscious, but still . . ."

Nicholas turned to Pointynog. "Snicknik is the only one fast enough. It has to be him."

"Fast enough to stand still?" Snicknik asked.

"What you said a moment ago," Nicholas said.

"Turn it around. You can go faster in your thoughts than in your body. And believe me, out there, your feet may be planted, but you'll hardly be standing still . . ."

A few minutes later, the storm was raging upon the spot where the helpless vessel had rocked and teetered—but it was gone!

The *Unity* soared to the coast of Dinotopia, outdistancing all but the light rains at the outskirts of the storm. The ship's remaining sails filled with the strong gusts of the tempest while the Liopleurodons hauled the vessel with all their strength and speed. A single figure stood on the back of the middle Liopleurodon—a knight without armor, a Troodon without fear.

Snicknik grasped the reins, responding to the signals given by each of the Liopleurodons. He had to constantly shift his stance, watch his balance, and send word with the lines he held to keep the great marine reptiles in formation. One would try to outdistance another, yet another might begin to sail below the surface, and another wandered from the pack.

Snicknik had to think before his every action, but he had to think on his feet, and he had to do it faster than he ever had before. There were no shortcuts here, but there was also no standing still, just as Nicholas had promised.

Looking back, Snicknik saw the steadily approaching wall of the storm. For a time, it seemed to be gaining. Snicknik wouldn't allow it. He pressed the Liopleurodons on, pushing them when he had to, allowing them to slow and pace themselves whenever he could.

The dark clouds and the raging thunder of the storm kept coming, but he howled in laughter and triumph anyway. Just like his ancestor, he was racing the wind!

On board, Nicholas stood with Pointynog and the other knights.

"Your punishment, when you return to Halcyon," Nicholas said. "Is there something I can say to this Lord Botolf? Some words that might sway him?"

"I'm not concerned," Pointynog said. "Not about that. Whether I'm a Knight of the Unrivaled or simply a wanderer, I've found my joy. I've explored a mystery. That is how I'll spend my life. I think my friends will join me in that quest."

Pointynog looked out at the shoreline in the far distance. They would make it to the docks before the storm was on them.

They had won.

He thought about the day he had stared Ironjaw in the face and said, What point is there to any contest other than winning or losing?

Now, finally, he understood the answer to that question. All life was a contest, a challenge. But the greatest moments of joy and truth came not from the outcome, but from the manner in which the challenge was met.

"All things really are possible," Nicholas said in wonder. "Tell me—why was the first Explorers Club formed?"

"Curiosity," Pointynog said. "It was my ancestor's idea. It was an age of mysteries, and he wanted to delve into those mysteries. To find the truth."

"Did he?"

"I'm told that he did. A truth, anyway. His truth. That's a thing that's different for everyone."

Nicholas looked away. "I know my truth. It isn't a thing that's easy to face."

"Nicholas, what were your dreams?" Pointynog asked urgently.

"My . . . dreams?"

"When you spoke with your father. When you told him what you wanted to do with your life. What was it you said?"

"It was foolishness," Nicholas said. "It is foolishness. Especially now."

"Nicholas, please."

The dolphinback let out a deep, shuddering breath. "I told him I wished to travel far and wide. I wished to go places no one had ever been. I dreamed of exploring mysteries and understanding the deeper meaning and shapes of things unknown. I wanted to know why people did what they did. I wanted to see wonders." He looked around. "And I have. Only—I've turned a blind eye to them. And I've done it one time too many. There's no going back."

"If you live in the present, every moment is a new beginning," Pointynog said.

Nicholas shook his head. "I don't understand."

"Hand in claw," Pointynog said as he reached out to Nicholas. "Every age is an age of mysteries. And in every place there can be found wonder. We five are explorers. It's the path we've chosen, not the one destiny had in store for us, no matter our names."

Nicholas shuddered. He hugged himself and did not look at the knight.

"Hand in claw, Nicholas," Pointynog said as he stepped closer.

At last, the young man looked up. There was fear and longing in his eyes.

Pointynog held out his gauntleted hand. "Will it be six?"

EPILOGUE

"And that's where our story leaves off," Lian said.

Alec bolted upright. "What? You can't stop there! What happened? Did Nicholas go with them? Was Pointynog punished? Was he still a knight? Did they have adventures? What?"

"All things are possible," Lian said. "What do you think happened?"

"I know what I wanted to happen," Alec said. The spark she had seen in his eyes faded. His features again turned dark.

Lian turned to the cave mouth. The soft, golden light of dawn streamed in. The acrid smell of the fire remained, yet . . .

From the cave mouth, Lian looked down into the valley. The worst of the fires were out. The school had been left untouched. Only a few barns at the far edge of their village had been seared by the flames.

"It's over," Lian said. "The fire has been contained."

Cheers rose about her as her students and the four

dinosaurs rushed to surround her. Only Alec remained. For an instant, his lower lip trembled, then he raised his chin and forced back his emotions. Lian had seen him do it a hundred times.

"He could have said yes," Alec said. "But things don't . . . People don't . . . "

Lian looked away.

In the distance, a small envoy approached. She could tell from the path they were on that they were among the many who had fought the blaze all night long. They appeared tired, but satisfied.

As they came closer, Lian smiled. "Alec, I think you'll want to see this."

With a sigh, Alec picked himself up and trudged over to the cave mouth. The sight that greeted him instantly infused him with energy and excitement. His back straightened and his eyes opened wide. He grabbed Lian's arm, shaking with happiness. It was the first time he had touched anyone in so enthusiastic a way since the dolphins had delivered him to the island.

"It's *them*," he said, his voice choked with emotion.

There were six in all. Five young Troodon knights in armor seared black from the flames—and one brave young lad whose hair was longer now, and whose leathers bore the same symbol of hand in claw as his companions.

One of the knights seemed to be laughing, another

lecturing, and still one other, who appeared far less tired than the rest, darted back and forth, practically running circles around his companions.

"Lian," Alec said, his voice trembling with emotion. "Can I—I mean, may I—"

"Why don't you go say hello?" Lian said. "We're all friends here."

With a joyous whoop, Alec raced down the hill toward the group of surprised but friendly explorers.

One of the knights raised his hand to Lian. With a few simple gestures known only to those who had trained with the knights of Halcyon, he told her that all was well. No lives had been lost battling the flames.

She bowed in thanks and watched with the others as Alec enthusiastically greeted the explorers.

No lives had been lost. And one had been regained.

ABOUT THE AUTHOR

SCOTT CIENCIN is a best-selling author of adult and children's fiction. Praised by *Science Fiction Review* as "one of today's finest fantasy writers," Scott has written over thirty works, many published by Warner, Avon, and TSR. For Random House Children's Publishing, Scott has been a favorite author in the popular *Dinotopia* series, for which he's written five other titles: *Windchaser, Lost City, Thunder Falls, Sky Dance,* and *Return to Lost City.*

"I grew up with a love of the fantastic," says Scott. "Being given the opportunity to write novels set in the world of James Gurney's Dinotopia put me on a path of discovery. In creating Dinotopia, James Gurney became the heir to the legacy of Jules Verne and other classic fantasists. Having the opportunity to add to the mythology he's created has not only made me a better writer, it's taught me lessons about the limitless vistas of the imagination."

Among Scott's other recent projects is the children's series *Dinoverse,* a six-book fantasy adventure that takes readers on an exciting and humorous journey through the Age of Dinosaurs. Scott's *Dinoverse* titles include: *I Was a Teenage T. Rex* (#1), *The Teens Time Forgot* (#2), *Raptor Without a Cause* (#3), *Please Don't Eat the Teacher!* (#4), *Beverly Hills Brontosaurus* (#5), and *Dinosaurs Ate My Homework* (#6).

In addition, Scott is the author of a newly launched series of original adventures set in Michael Crichton's fictional world of Jurassic Park. The first books in the *Jurassic Park Adventures* series are *Survivor* (#1), *Prey* (#2), and *Flyers* (#3). Scott has also directed for television and scripted comic books. He lives in Florida with his wife, Denise.

DRIVING FORCES:
Motor Vehicle Trends and Their Implications for Global Warming, Energy Strategies, and Transportation Planning

James J. MacKenzie
Michael P. Walsh

WORLD RESOURCES INSTITUTE

December 1990

Kathleen Courrier
Publications Director

Brooks Clapp
Marketing Manager

Hyacinth Billings
Production Manager

Tommy Noonan for *Mass Transit* (1974)
Cover Photo

Each World Resources Institute Report represents a timely, scientific treatment of a subject of public concern. WRI takes responsibility for choosing the study topics and guaranteeing its authors and researchers freedom of inquiry. It also solicits and responds to the guidance of advisory panels and expert reviewers. Unless otherwise stated, however, all the interpretation and findings set forth in WRI publications are those of the authors.

Contents

Acknowledgments

This report has enjoyed warm support and input from WRI's Policy Panel on Responses to the Greenhouse Effect and Global Climate Change. We would like to specifically thank Panel members Gordon MacDonald, Robert Stafford, George Woodwell, and George Rathjens, for providing comments on an earlier draft.

The report has also benefited greatly from the generous and thoughtful comments of many colleagues. From within WRI we thank Jessica Mathews, Roger Dower, Allen Hammond, Robert Repetto and Bill Moomaw (now at Tufts University). Outside reviewers include Debbie Bleviss, Barry McNutt, Steve Plotkin, Debbie Gordon, Nick Lenssen, Mike Schwarz, Tom Burke, Peter Sand, and Timothy O'Riordan—to all of whom we express our gratitude. Ultimately, of course, the authors alone are responsible for the accuracy and recommendations of the report.

Our special thanks to Kathleen Courrier for her skillful editing of the report, to Robbie Nichols for her editing and writing assistance, to Hyacinth Billings for preparing the text and Allyn Massey for preparing the figures, to Sue Terry for helping us obtain numerous reports and references, and to Margot Greenlee and Cindy Barger for their day-to-day support while this study was underway.

Finally, our gratitude to WRI President Gus Speth and Senior Vice President Mohamed El-Ashry for their overall guidance and continuing support.

J.J.M.
M.P.W.

Foreword

Our aggravated assault on the atmosphere is one of our century's most damaging environmental legacies—and our love of cars has a lot to do with it. Ozone depletion and global warming both threaten undesirable changes over coming decades, and both are exacerbated by petroleum-powered vehicles. Meanwhile, the Persian Gulf crisis is driving home a more immediate threat, the economic and security risks of continued dependence on Mideast oil, most of which is used in transportation.

Cars, trucks, and other vehicles have long been linked to smog and other urban pollution, but the part they play in the larger complex of atmospheric and energy ills that we now face is often overlooked. In *Driving Forces: Motor Vehicle Trends and Their Implications for Global Warming, Energy Strategies, and Transportation Planning*, James J. MacKenzie, senior associate in World Resources Institute's Program in Climate, Energy, and Pollution, and Michael P. Walsh, an international consultant on transportation and environmental issues, fill in this knowledge gap with new data and analyses. The report focuses especially on the United States, which pioneered the automotive revolution and leads the world in oil imports and emissions.

In this country, motor vehicles account for a quarter of all fossil-fuel generated carbon dioxide, and auto air conditioning is the largest single source of chlorofluorocarbons (CFCs).

Globally, the motor vehicle fleet, now at 500 million strong, accounts for some 14 percent of carbon dioxide emissions from fuel burning. That may not sound so bad until you realize that the fleet is expected to double to one billion over the next twenty to forty years.

What can be done to mitigate transportation's impact on climate? Efficiency measures and pollution controls could help for several decades. But if the motor vehicle population and the mileage it logs keep growing at expected rates, benefits that are within our grasp today will be out of reach tomorrow. Only with an international push to reduce fuel use and pollution, while at the same time making transportation systems more efficient and developing new kinds of transport that emit no greenhouse gases whatever, can we prove equal to the challenge.

MacKenzie and Walsh spell out four policy shifts that can help hold the line on global warming:

1. Improve New-Vehicle Efficiency. When world oil prices collapsed during the 1980s, new-car fuel efficiency fell and tailpipe emissions rose. The long-term effects of the current Persian Gulf crisis on oil prices and fuel efficiency remain to be seen, but complacency would be foolhardy, especially when such heroic efforts are needed to lessen dependency. Greatly improving new-vehicle fuel efficiency and encouraging the phaseout of older, less efficient cars and trucks would do much to reduce vehicular carbon dioxide emissions. Fortunately, much of the technology needed to produce more efficient vehicles has already been demonstrated in ultra-efficient ''concept'' cars that get up to 100 miles per gallon of gasoline.

2. Make Transportation More Efficient. Convenient, affordable public transport would cut carbon dioxide emissions and also break up traffic gridlock, cut road fatalities, and make the air more breathable. Policies that encourage commuters to use van and car pools, buses, trolleys, and trains and discourage driving alone to and from work would make an enormous difference. There would still be plenty of urban traffic, but better management could keep it moving—and thus save energy.

3. Cut Other Greenhouse Gas Emissions. Half of all new cars have state-of-the-art pollution controls, but the car population boom has wiped out reductions in per-car pollution. Requiring advanced pollution controls on *all* vehicles would for a few decades limit growth in carbon monoxide, hydrocarbon, and nitrogen oxide emissions—all of which contribute indirectly to the greenhouse problem. Cradle-to-grave controls on CFCs—the most potent greenhouse gases, and ozone-destroyers to boot—are especially needed.

4. Create the Green Car of the Future. Technical improvements in petroleum-powered vehicles can help for now, but they will not be enough over the long haul. Ultimately, the world needs non-polluting cars that run on something other than fossil fuels, and the mass-production of such cars ought to become a high priority in the United States, Japan, and Europe—the three leading auto-makers. Mercedes-Benz and BMW have already produced hydrogen-powered vehicles for research use. General Motors is now selling an electric van, and Chrysler's electric mini-van could roll off the assembly lines as early as 1993. Limited fuel storage restricts the range of today's hydrogen- and electricity-powered cars, but stepping up research could overcome such constraints.

Driving Forces is the latest in the World Resources Institute's continuing series of reports on climate, energy, and pollution policies. This report's recommendations extend those of such previous studies as *Breathing Easier: Taking Action on Climate Change, Air Pollution, and Energy Insecurity; Ill Winds: Airborne Pollution's Toll on Trees and Crops; A Matter of Degrees: The Potential for Limiting the Greenhouse Effect;* and *The Sky is the Limit: Strategies for Protecting the Ozone Layer.*

Driving Forces owes an intellectual debt to the leading experts in international relations, climatology, agriculture, energy, environment, law, trade, industry, and the developing world who serve on WRI's Policy Panel on Responses to the Greenhouse Effect and Global Climate Change. In several meetings over the past two years, the panel deliberated at length over the future of transportation in general and the automobile in particular. Its members offered comments and recommendations crucial to analyses contained in *Driving Forces,* and their assistance is highly valued.

Financial support for WRI's work on transportation and other climate and energy issues has been provided by The Joyce Foundation, The Nathan Cummings Foundation, The Ford Foundation, The Andrew W. Mellon Foundation, Public Welfare Foundation, Inc., Rockefeller Brothers Fund, and Sasakawa Peace Foundation. To all these institutions, we express our deep appreciation.

James Gustave Speth
President
World Resources Institute

WORLD RESOURCES INSTITUTE
POLICY PANEL ON
RESPONSES TO
THE GREENHOUSE EFFECT AND GLOBAL CLIMATE CHANGE

Mr. Richard E. Ayres
Senior Staff Attorney
Natural Resources Defense Council

Ambassador Richard E. Benedick
Senior Fellow
World Wildlife Fund/The Conservation
Foundation

Mr. Harold Corbett
Senior Vice President
The Monsanto Company

Dr. John Firor
Director, Advanced Study Program
National Center for Atmospheric Research

Dr. Richard Gardner
Professor of Law and International
Organization
Columbia University School of Law

Margaret L. Kripke, MD
Professor & Chairman
Department of Immunology
University of Texas

Mr. C. Payne Lucas
Executive Director
AFRICARE

Dr. Gordon J. MacDonald
Vice President and Chief Scientist
The MITRE Corporation

Dr. Jessica Tuchman Mathews
Vice President
World Resources Institute

Mr. Robert McNamara
Former President, the World Bank

Mr. William G. Miller
President
The American Committee on U.S.-Soviet
Relations

Dr. Michael Oppenheimer
Senior Scientist
Environmental Defense Fund

Dr. George Rathjens
Center for International Studies
Massachusetts Institute of Technology

Mr. Roger Sant
Chairman
Applied Energy Services

Dr. Maxine Savitz
Director, Garrett Ceramic Components Division
Garrett Processing Company

Dr. Joseph J. Sisco
Sisco Associates

Mr. James Gustave Speth
President
World Resources Institute

I. Introduction

The disruption of world oil supply in the wake of Iraq's invasion of Kuwait illustrates once again the security and economic risks that oil-consuming nations run by relying on the troubled Persian Gulf for a significant portion of their energy. But unless these countries—especially the industrialized democracies—can suppress their appetite for oil, they will not be able to cut their imports from this volatile region. The United States, Canada, Western Europe, and Japan consume well over half of the oil produced in the world annually but contribute less than a quarter of world supply. Increasingly, the gap between their domestic supply and demand will be made up by OPEC producers, particularly by the Persian Gulf producers who together control two thirds of the earth's proven oil reserves.

Worldwide, the issues related to oil demand and supply are inextricably connected to ground transportation. Globally, motor vehicles—powered almost universally by oil—account for a third of world oil consumption. In the OECD* countries, they represent over 40 percent of demand and in the United States, over 50 percent. Clearly, any long-term international perspective on transportation must recognize that security of fuel supply is destined to become an increasingly urgent issue in the years ahead.

Apart from their role in increasing dependence on foreign oil, motor vehicles pose other risks to modern societies as well. Motor vehicles are major sources of several health-threatening air pollutants as well as carbon dioxide, the most important of the greenhouse gases.

Examining the long-term effects of motor vehicle emissions on the atmosphere—and on global warming in particular—leads to some unsettling conclusions. In general, if motor vehicle use continues rising as it has over the last two decades, petroleum consumption and carbon dioxide emissions will increase too. As these emissions grow, slowing global warming becomes ever more difficult. As this report makes clear, reducing the long-term risks of pollution and climate change will require fundamental changes in transportation technology and planning that need to be fully reflected in the development of national energy and transportation policies.

Unfortunately, no tidy solution is at hand, and even certain necessary changes—namely

---

*Full members of the Organization for Economic Cooperation and Development include Australia, Austria, Belgium, Canada, Denmark, Finland, France, West Germany, Greece, Iceland, Ireland, Italy, Japan, Luxembourg, the Netherlands, New Zealand, Norway, Portugal, Spain, Sweden, Switzerland, Turkey, the United Kingdom, and the United States. Yugoslavia also participates in some OECD activities.

vehicle efficiency improvements—cannot by themselves blunt the thrust of increased growth in the use of motor vehicles. This preliminary analysis does make it clear, however, that the introduction of new technologies and improved transportation planning will be essential elements in any long-term response to climate change, dependence on foreign oil, and air pollution.

II. The Global Warming Problem

Over the past century, huge amounts of air pollutants and gases have been released into the atmosphere that now pose risks to human health, natural ecosystems, and the earth's climate.[1] Many kinds of industrial and agricultural activities have contributed to these releases. Fossil fuel combustion, massive deforestation, the release of industrial chemicals, and agricultural development have amplified the natural greenhouse effect, increasing the risk of global warming. In addition, the release of industrial chemicals containing chlorine and bromine has contributed to the depletion of the ozone layer,[2] and fuel burning and industrial development account for most of the planet's air pollution, including acid rain and urban smog.

Motor vehicles contribute to both the build-up of greenhouse gases—potentially the most serious of these problems—and the creation of smog and acid rain. The predicted growth in the worldwide use of cars, trucks, and other ground-level vehicles portends growing conflicts between a continuation of past patterns of development and the crucial need to protect and enhance the environment and public health.

Greenhouse warming occurs when certain gases allow sunlight to penetrate to the earth but partially trap the planet's radiated infrared heat in the atmosphere. Some such warming is natural and necessary.[3] If there were no water vapor, carbon dioxide, methane, and other infrared-absorbing (greenhouse) gases in the atmosphere trapping the earth's radiant heat, our planet would be about 60°F (33°C) colder, and life as we know it would not be possible.

Over the past century, however, human activities have increased atmospheric concentrations of naturally occurring greenhouse gases and added new and very powerful infrared-absorbing gases to the mixture. Even more disturbing, in recent decades the atmosphere has begun to change through human activities at dramatically accelerated rates. According to a growing scientific consensus, if current emissions trends continue, the atmospheric build-up of greenhouse gases released by fossil fuel burning, as well as industrial, agricultural, and forestry activities, is likely to turn our benign atmospheric "greenhouse" into a progressively warmer "heat trap," as Norway's Prime Minister, Ms. Gro Harlem Brundtland, recently termed this overheating.

How much do various human endeavors contribute to climate change? As recent estimates by the World Resources Institute (WRI) show,[4] by far the largest contributor (about 50 percent) is energy consumption, mostly from the burning of fossil fuels. (See Figure 1.) Chlorofluorocarbons (CFCs), the second largest contributor to global warming, account for about 20 percent of the total. Mostly known for depleting the stratospheric ozone layer, these stable, long-lived chemicals are also extremely

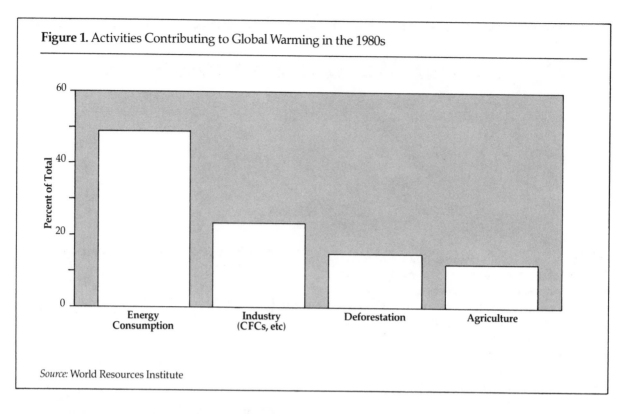

Figure 1. Activities Contributing to Global Warming in the 1980s

Percent of Total

Energy Consumption | Industry (CFCs, etc) | Deforestation | Agriculture

Source: World Resources Institute

potent greenhouse gases. Deforestation and agricultural activities (such as rice production, cattle raising, and the use of nitrogen fertilizers) each contribute about 13 to 14 percent to global warming.

WRI estimates for current contributions to global warming from the most important greenhouse gases are shown in Figure 2. Carbon dioxide (CO_2) accounts for about half of the annual increase in global warming. The atmospheric concentration of carbon dioxide, now growing at about 0.5 percent per year, has already increased by about 25 percent since preindustrial times. Half of this increase has occurred over just the past three decades.

Globally, about two thirds of anthropogenic carbon dioxide emissions arise from fossil-fuel burning, the rest primarily from deforestation. In the United States, electric power plants account for about 33 percent of carbon dioxide emissions, followed by motor vehicles, planes, and ships (31 percent), industrial plants (24

percent), and commercial and residential buildings (11 percent).

Globally, about two thirds of anthropogenic carbon dioxide emissions arise from fossil-fuel burning, the rest primarily from deforestation.

The third largest contributor (after the CFCs) is methane (CH_4), accounting for about 13 to 18 percent of the total warming.[5] Sources of this culprit gas include anaerobic decay in bogs, swamps, and other wetlands; rice growing; livestock production; termites; biomass burning; fossil fuel production and use; and landfills.[6] Methane may also be arising from the warming of the frozen Arctic tundra. The atmospheric concentration of methane is growing by about 1 percent annually.

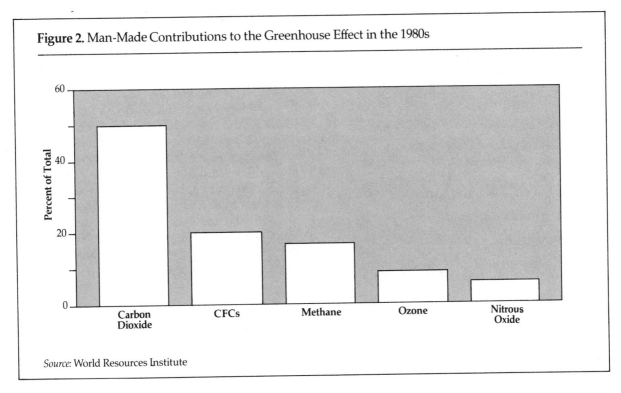

Figure 2. Man-Made Contributions to the Greenhouse Effect in the 1980s

Source: World Resources Institute

Ozone (O_3) in the lower atmosphere (the troposphere) is the principal ingredient of smog. This gas is created in sunlight-driven reactions involving nitrogen oxides, NO_x (as distinct from nitrous oxide, N_2O) given off when either fossil fuels or biomass are burned, and volatile organic compounds from a wide spectrum of anthropogenic and natural sources. In Western Europe, road transportation accounts for an estimated 50 to 70 percent of NO_x emissions and almost half of anthropogenic emissions of organic compounds.[7] In the United States, highway vehicles are the source of about 31 percent of NO_x emissions and about 44 percent of volatile organic compounds. Tropospheric ozone contributes about 8 percent to global warming.

Exactly where nitrous oxide (N_2O) comes from is still uncertain, but prime suspects include the use of agricultural fertilizers and, perhaps, the burning of biomass and coal. Nitrous oxide accounts for about 6 percent of current enhanced warming[8] and also contributes to depletion of the stratospheric ozone layer.

As greenhouse gases accumulate in the atmosphere, they amplify the earth's natural greenhouse effect, profoundly and perhaps irreversibly threatening all humankind and the natural environment. While most scientists agree on the overall features of such warming, considerable uncertainties still surround its timing, magnitude, and regional impacts.[9] Major unanswered questions include whether the additional clouds that are likely to form will have a net cooling or warming effect, how the sources and sinks of greenhouse gases will change, and whether the polar and Greenland ice sheets will grow or retreat. At any rate, the complexity of the global climate system is daunting and the interactions between the atmosphere and the oceans are still imperfectly understood.

Unless measures are soon taken to reduce the release of greenhouse gases, by as early as 2030 they could reach levels equivalent to twice the carbon dioxide concentrations of pre-industrial times.[10] According to the most informed scientific opinion, continued ''business-as-usual" growth in greenhouse gas emissions will lead to

- an increase in the global average temperature of 2 degrees Celsius (3.6 degrees F), with a range of 1.4 to 2.8 degrees Celsius (2.5 to 5 degrees F), over preindustrial levels by the year 2030;[11]

- sea-level rises great enough to threaten wetlands, accelerate coastal erosion, exacerbate coastal flooding, and increase the salinity of estuaries and aquifers;[12]

- changes in rainfall patterns;

- more intense tropical storms;

- more severe droughts, especially in mid-continental regions, resulting in dislocations and reduced agricultural output; and

- the loss of many unmanaged ecosystems.

Some of these changes could be gradual. The United Nations-sponsored Intergovernmental Panel on Climate Change (IPCC) recently estimated that sea levels may rise an average of 6 to 20 inches above current levels by 2050 if present trends continue.[13] However, the totally unanticipated opening of the Antarctic ozone hole heightens scientists' anxiety about how quickly such significant and poorly understood phenomena can develop. Many experts fear that climate changes, once initiated, could occur faster than expected.

III. How Motor Vehicles Contribute to Global Warming and Air Pollution

Worldwide, cars, trucks, buses, and other motor vehicles are playing an ever increasing role in global climate change and air pollution.* As large oil consumers, motor vehicles are major sources of carbon dioxide; volatile organic compounds (VOCs) and nitrogen oxides, the precursors to both tropospheric ozone and acid rain; carbon monoxide (CO); and chlorofluorocarbons (CFCs).[14] All of these gases contribute to greenhouse warming either directly or indirectly; CFCs also contribute to depletion of the stratospheric ozone layer.

Carbon Dioxide from Vehicles

Virtually the entire global motor vehicle fleet runs on fossil fuels, primarily oil. For every gallon of oil consumed by a motor vehicle, about 19 pounds of carbon dioxide (containing about 5.3 pounds of carbon) go directly into the atmosphere.** In other words, for every 15-gallon fill-up at the service station, about 300 pounds of carbon dioxide are eventually released into the atmosphere. Globally, motor vehicles account for about a third of world oil consumption and about 14 percent of the

---

*Aircraft and ships are also important sources of carbon dioxide and air pollution, but this report covers only ground vehicles.
**Direct tail-pipe emissions only. Transportation, refining, and distribution account for perhaps 15 to 20 percent of total emissions.

world's carbon dioxide emissions from fossil fuel burning. For the United States, the figures are 50 percent of oil demand and about 25 percent of carbon dioxide emissions.

Tropospheric Ozone

Although ozone in the lower atmosphere does not come directly from motor vehicles, they are the major source of ozone precursors throughout the industrialized world. Over the past 100 years, "background" ozone levels have approximately doubled,[15] and monitoring data suggest that ozone concentrations are increasing by about 1 percent per year in the northern hemisphere.[16]

Historically, EPA's strategy for reducing the concentrations of ozone (the principal ingredient of smog) has been to tightly restrict volatile organic compound (VOC) emissions. But, recent research indicates, further controls of nitrogen oxides releases may also be needed.[17] Without them, the continued emission of nitrogen oxides will increase ozone problems in downwind rural areas and some urban areas. Controls of nitrogen oxides are also needed to reduce the deposition of nitric acid, an important component of acid rain.

Besides contributing to the greenhouse problem, ozone pollution also adversely affects human health, crops, other vegetation, and materials. Eye irritation, coughing and chest

7

discomfort, headaches, upper respiratory illness, increased asthma attacks, and reduced pulmonary function can all plague people exposed to ozone.[18] This gas has also been shown to reduce crop productivity, with U.S. annual losses of several billion dollars, and to kill ponderosa and Jeffrey pines in California and eastern white pines in the eastern United States.[19]

About 112 million Americans reside in areas where the current air quality standard is violated.

Widespread and pervasive, smog looks to be a long-term problem in many areas of the world unless more stringent controls are adopted. About 112 million Americans reside in areas where the current air quality standard is violated.[20]

Carbon Monoxide

Carbon monoxide—an odorless, invisible gas created when fuels containing carbon are burned incompletely—poses a serious threat to human health. Participating in various chemical reactions in the atmosphere, it also contributes to smog formation and the buildup of methane.

Exposure to carbon monoxide results primarily from motor vehicle emissions, though in some locales wood burning is also an important source. People with coronary artery disease who are exposed to carbon monoxide during exercise experience chest pain (angina); exposure also alters their electrocardiograms.[21] Although ambient carbon monoxide levels have been reduced across Europe, Japan, and the United States, the problem is far from under control. In 44 major U.S. metropolitan areas with a combined population of some 30 million people, the national carbon monoxide air quality standard is currently not being met.[22]

Global carbon monoxide concentrations in the lower atmosphere are increasing by between 0.8 percent and 1.4 percent per year.[23] For the five countries for which data on carbon monoxide emissions are available, transportation accounted for 59 to 84 percent of releases.[24] In the United States, 67 percent of the carbon monoxide emissions in 1988 came from transportation.[25]

Carbon monoxide can elevate concentrations of tropospheric ozone and methane in several ways. First, carbon monoxide helps convert nitric oxide (NO) to nitrogen dioxide (NO_2)—a crucial step in ozone formation.[26] Second, the hydroxyl radical (OH) that eventually removes carbon monoxide from the atmosphere is also the principal chemical that destroys ozone and methane. If carbon monoxide levels increase, OH concentrations will fall and regional concentrations of ozone and methane will rise.

Reliable data are not available on global air pollution emissions from transportation activities. For the twenty-four OECD countries, however, motor vehicles are the dominant source of emissions of carbon monoxide, oxides of nitrogen, and volatile organic compounds. *(See Table 1.)*

Table 1. Motor Vehicle Share of OECD Pollutant Emissions (1000 tons, 1980)

Pollutant	Total Emissions	M-V Share
NO_x	36,019	17,012 (47%)
HC	33,869	13,239 (39%)
CO	119,148	78,227 (66%)

Source: OECD Environmental Data, Organization for Economic Cooperation and Development, Paris, 1987.

8

Chlorofluorocarbons (CFCs)

Highly potent greenhouse gases, CFCs also reduce the protective stratospheric ozone layer.[27] During the Antarctic spring, the ozone hole spans an area the size of North America. At certain altitudes over the Antarctic, the ozone is destroyed almost completely.

If CFCs continue to deplete the world's stratospheric ozone layer, ultraviolet radiation would increase and so would ground-level ozone formation. Even a moderate loss in the total ozone column would significantly boost peak ozone levels at the earth's surface. By allowing more ultraviolet radiation through the ozone shield, such a loss is also expected to increase the number of skin cancers and impair the human immune system. Increased ultraviolet radiation might also harm the life-supporting plankton that dwell in the ocean's upper levels, thus jeopardizing marine food chains that depend on the tiny plankton.

A major source of CFCs in the atmosphere is motor-vehicle air conditioning, and in 1987 approximately 48 percent of all new cars, trucks, and buses manufactured worldwide were equipped with air conditioners.[28] (CFCs also are used as a blowing agent in the production of seating and other foam products, but this is a considerably smaller vehicular use.) Annually, about 120,000 metric tons of CFCs are used in new vehicles and in servicing air conditioners in older vehicles. In all, these uses account for about 28 percent of global demand for CFC-12. According to EPA, in the United States, vehicular air conditioners are the single largest users of CFCs, accounting for about 54,000 metric tons of CFC-12 demand in 1985[29] and roughly 16 percent of total U.S. CFC use in 1989.[30] (See Table 2.) As agreed under the Montreal Protocol, CFCs are to be completely phased out of new vehicles by the turn of the century.

Table 2. Estimated U.S. Consumption of CFC-12 for Mobile Air Conditioning (1000 tons)

Use	CFC Consumption	% of Total
Initial charge of units		
US	14.7	27.2
Imported	2.8	5.2
Aftermarket	1.0	1.8
Recharge of Units		
After leakage	13.5	25.0
After service venting	18.2	33.6
After accident	3.9	7.2
TOTALS	54.1	100.0

Source: "Regulatory Impact Analysis: Protection of Stratospheric Ozone," Environmental Protection Agency, Washington, D.C., December, 1987.

IV. Historic and Projected Vehicle Use and Carbon Dioxide Emissions

In 1950, there were about 53 million cars on the world's roads, 76 percent of them in the United States. Only four decades later, the global automobile fleet is over 400 million, an almost eightfold increase. On average, the fleet has grown by about 9 million automobiles per year. Outside the United States, the growth in automobiles has been especially high, rising from slightly under 13 million in 1950 to more than 270 million in 1988, a growth rate of more than 8 percent per year.[31] While the growth rate has slowed in the highly industrialized countries, population growth and increased urbanization and industrialization are accelerating the use of motor vehicles elsewhere.

Trends in World Motor Vehicle Production

Figure 3 summarizes the worldwide trends in the production of both cars and other motor vehicles since 1900. Overall growth in production, especially since the end of World War II, has been dramatic, rising from about 5 million motor vehicles per year to almost 50 million. Between 1950 and 1989, production increased almost linearly from about 10 million vehicles per year to about 49.5 million per year. *(See Figure 4.)* With the 1990 upheaval in the Middle East, the future of world oil prices has become quite uncertain, casting into doubt the future growth rate in vehicle production and use.

Over the past several decades, motor vehicle production has shifted away from North America. *(See Figure 5.)* The first wave of competition came from Europe, and by the late 1960s European production had surpassed that of the United States. Over the past two decades the car industry in Asia, led by Japan, has grown rapidly and now rivals both those in the United States and Europe.

As Table 3 shows, the dominance of the United States and Germany and, to a much greater extent, the United Kingdom, in motor vehicle manufacturing, has slipped over the past two decades. At the same time, the market share enjoyed by Spain, Korea, and, especially, Japan has grown dramatically. These rankings are based on the number of motor vehicles actually manufactured within the countries.

Of the more than 48 million vehicles manufactured in 1988, over 70 percent were produced by the top 10 manufacturers. The top 14 produced 80 percent. *(See Table 4.)* Thirty other manufacturers made most of the rest. As a result of this market concentration, efforts to reduce the global climate impacts of motor vehicle use could, in principle, be achieved through negotiations with, or regulation of, a relatively few corporations. Of the top fourteen motor vehicle manufacturers, three are American, six are Japanese, two West German, two French, and one Italian. (In this accounting, vehicles are counted by company, regardless of

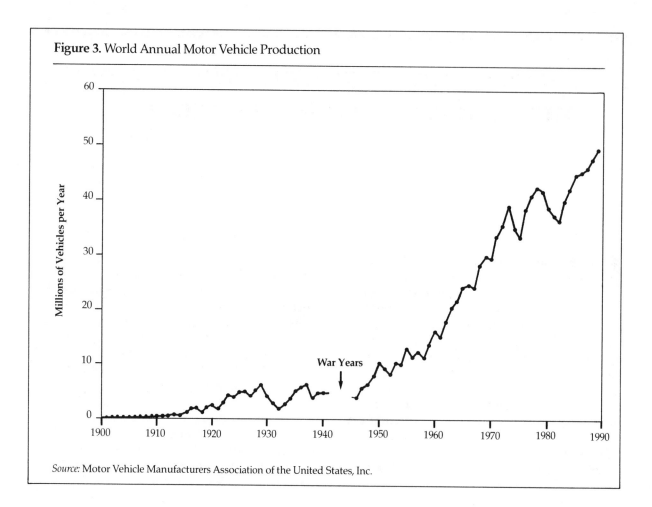

Figure 3. World Annual Motor Vehicle Production

Millions of Vehicles per Year

War Years

Source: Motor Vehicle Manufacturers Association of the United States, Inc.

Table 3. Ranking of Western Motor Vehicle Producing Countries, 1965, 1975, 1985, and 1989 (Measured by total production within the country)

Country	1965	1975	1985	1989	Country	1965	1975	1985	1989
United States	1	1	2	2	Australia	8	10	10	13
West Germany	2	3	3	3	Spain	9	9	8	6
United Kingdom	3	5	7	8	Sweden	10	11	11	12
Japan	4	2	1	1	Brazil	11	8	9	10
France	5	4	4	4	Mexico	12	12	12	11
Italy	6	6	6	5	Republic of Korea	13	13	13	9
Canada	7	7	5	7					

Source: Automotive News, Market Data Book (1986, 1990) Issues.

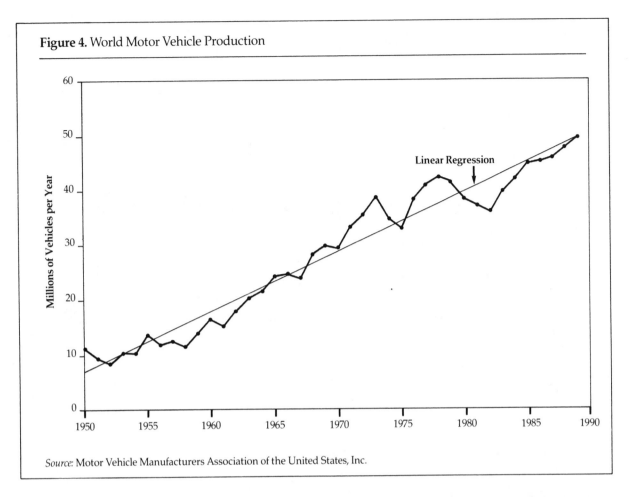

Figure 4. World Motor Vehicle Production

Source: Motor Vehicle Manufacturers Association of the United States, Inc.

where the vehicles were manufactured or assembled.) In 1988, North American companies manufactured 34 percent of all motor vehicles. Japanese companies placed second with 29 percent, and Western Europe third with 25 percent.

As Figure 6 shows, Japan's gains in non-passenger (commercial) vehicle production since 1975 rival the country's gains in passenger car manufacturing. As a result, in 1989 Japan was the world's largest motor vehicle manufacturer (measured by the total number of vehicles manufactured within the country), ahead of the United States and Europe. (Countries can be ranked according to their motor vehicle production in two distinctly different ways. The first is based on the total number of vehicles actually manufactured within the

borders of the country. By this measure, Japan is first. The second is based on the total number of vehicles manufactured by corporations headquartered within a country. According to this measure, U.S. manufacturers are still number one, largely because of overseas production.)

As for worldwide vehicle registrations, the long-term trends are upward, though the vehicle mix is slowly changing. *(See Figure 7.)* In 1950, trucks of all kinds and buses represented about 25 percent of all vehicles on the road. Their share dropped to about 21 percent of the total in 1970 but had edged back up to about 24 percent by 1988. Registrations of vehicles other than passenger cars have been growing for several decades by about 4.1 million vehicles per year; car registrations have been

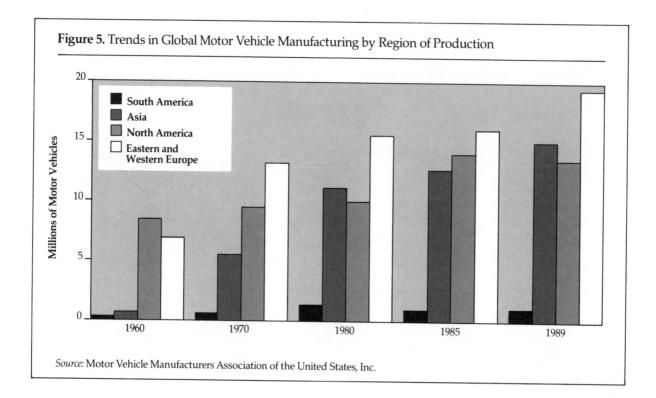

Figure 5. Trends in Global Motor Vehicle Manufacturing by Region of Production

Source: Motor Vehicle Manufacturers Association of the United States, Inc.

Table 4. Ranking of World Motor Vehicle Manufacturers (1988)
(Includes vehicles manufactured in other countries)

	Production (Millions)	Percent	Cumulative %
1. General Motors, U.S.	7.743	16.1	16.1
2. Ford Motor, U.S.	6.227	12.9	29.0
3. Toyota, Japan	4.084	8.5	37.5
4. Volkswagen, W. Germany	2.875	6.0	43.5
5. Nissan, Japan	2.700	5.6	49.1
6. Peugeot-Citroen, France	2.465	5.1	54.2
7. Chrysler, U.S.	2.338	4.9	59.1
8. Renault, France	2.102	4.4	63.5
9. Fiat, Italy	2.050	4.3	67.8
10. Honda, Japan	1.709	3.5	71.3
11. Mazda, Japan	1.384	2.9	74.2
12. Mitsubishi, Japan	1.261	2.6	76.8
13. Suzuki, Japan	0.846	1.8	78.6
14. Daimler-Benz, W. Germany	0.802	1.7	80.3

Source: ''World Motor Vehicle Data,'' 1990 Edition, Motor Vehicle Manufacturers Association of the United States, Inc., Page 16.

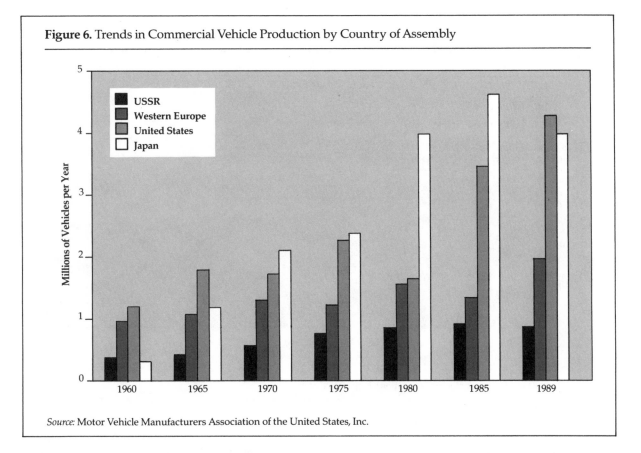

Figure 6. Trends in Commercial Vehicle Production by Country of Assembly

Millions of Vehicles per Year

Legend:
- USSR
- Western Europe
- United States
- Japan

(x-axis years: 1960, 1965, 1970, 1975, 1980, 1985, 1989)

Source: Motor Vehicle Manufacturers Association of the United States, Inc.

growing almost three times as fast. If both growth rates continue, over the long term three of every four motor vehicles on the road will be passenger cars.

Motor vehicle registrations for 1988 for various parts of the world are displayed in Figure 8. Europe (including Eastern Europe and the USSR) and North America each have about 40 percent of the world's motor vehicle population. The remainder is divided among Asia, South America, Africa, and Oceania (Australia, New Zealand, and Guam), in that order. North America has about 40 percent of the world's trucks and buses, followed closely by Asia and then Europe.

By any reckoning, North America and Western Europe are the dominant markets for new motor vehicles, primarily because these countries have large fleets and many of their

North America and Western Europe are the dominant markets for new motor vehicles, primarily because these countries have large fleets and many of their vehicles are scrapped—and replaced—each year.

vehicles are scrapped—and replaced—each year. For example, while the total number of registered motor vehicles in the United States grew by only 4.4 million (a 2.5-percent increase) between 1987 and 1988, more than 11 million vehicles were retired from use.[32] Thus, total U.S. motor-vehicle sales in 1988—taking

15

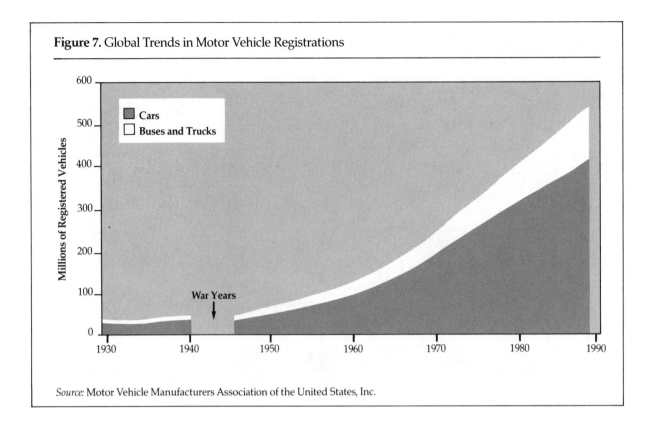

Figure 7. Global Trends in Motor Vehicle Registrations

Source: Motor Vehicle Manufacturers Association of the United States, Inc.

into account both new and replacement vehicles—were almost 16 million units, about a third of total world production for 1988. Because of this "turnover" effect, countries with large motor vehicle fleets also account for a large fraction of world sales.

In terms of per capita motor vehicle registration for various regions, the United States, Japan, and Europe also account for the lion's share of the ownership and use of motor vehicles. *(See Figure 9.)* Indeed, Africa and Asia (excluding Japan) are home to nearly three fourths of the world's population, yet account for only 12 percent of world motor-vehicle registrations.[33]

These registration patterns make it clear that the industrialized countries basically both control and dominate the world motor vehicle market today and probably will for the foreseeable future. For this reason, the design of

vehicles sold in the developed countries will greatly influence the design of those sold elsewhere. If, for example, emission controls or fuel economy requirements were tightened in the industrialized democracies, similar requirements would most likely be adopted in countries looking to export motor vehicles to the industrialized countries. By the same token, if requirements in the industrialized nations are weak, those throughout the rest of the world probably will be too.

Changes in new-car designs in the developed countries have impacts that extend far beyond the "useful life" of the vehicles. Once removed from service in industrialized countries, many older vehicles are exported to the developing world. The vehicle standards adopted in the industrialized nations thus influence pollution emissions and fuel use in industrializing countries for many years to come.

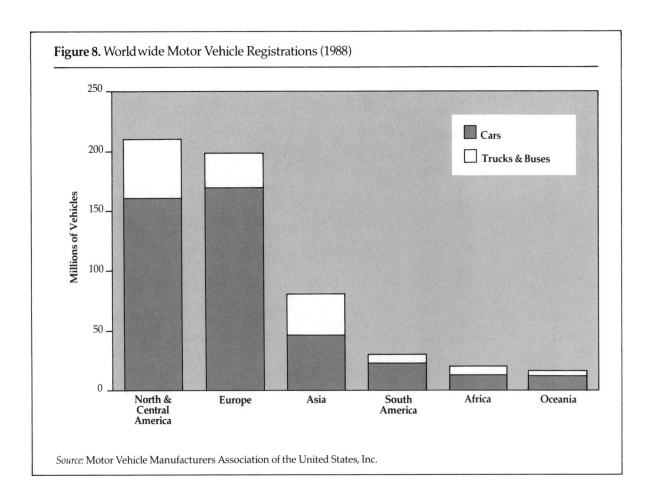

Figure 8. Worldwide Motor Vehicle Registrations (1988)

Millions of Vehicles

Legend: Cars, Trucks & Buses

North & Central America, Europe, Asia, South America, Africa, Oceania

Source: Motor Vehicle Manufacturers Association of the United States, Inc.

Trends in Motor Vehicle Carbon Dioxide Emissions

Fuel consumption and carbon dioxide emissions from motor vehicles have grown along with the global vehicle population and the number of vehicle-miles traveled.[34] As Figure 10 shows, vehicular carbon dioxide emissions rose, on average, by 3 percent per year from about 510 million tons of carbon in 1971 to over 830 million tons in 1987. Currently, global carbon dioxide emissions from vehicles increase by about 19 million metric tons of carbon per year. Of this amount, about 10.4 million tons come from the OECD countries and 8.7 million from all other nations combined.

The 63-percent increase in motor-vehicle carbon dioxide emissions between 1971 and 1987 is significantly less than the nearly 87-percent increase in the number of vehicles—presumably reflecting an overall improvement in the fuel efficiency of the global fleet. At the same time, the relative contribution of motor vehicles to global carbon dioxide emissions has been gradually increasing. In 1971, motor vehicles accounted for only about 12 percent of total global carbon dioxide emissions from fossil fuel combustion. By 1985, the percentage stood at about 14 percent.

Comparatively, how much do the United States and other regions contribute to motor

17

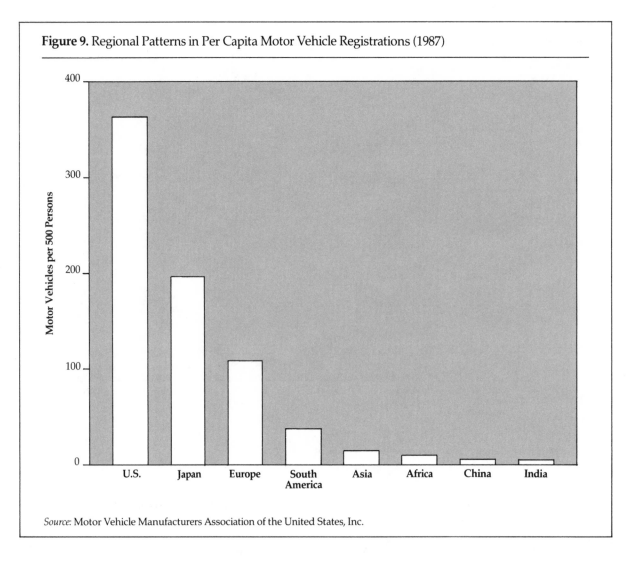

Figure 9. Regional Patterns in Per Capita Motor Vehicle Registrations (1987)

Source: Motor Vehicle Manufacturers Association of the United States, Inc.

vehicle carbon dioxide emissions? As Figure 11 shows, the United States and other OECD countries accounted for fully 77 percent of all motor vehicle carbon dioxide emissions in 1971. The United States alone accounted for 48 percent of the total. By 1987, the OECD contribution had declined to about 69 percent of the total and the United States to about 38 percent. The rest of the world's share—the portion that is increasing most rapidly today—rose from 23 percent to 31 percent.

Apart from shifts in their relative shares, each of these three groups of countries substantially increased its carbon dioxide emissions between 1971 and 1987. U.S. emissions increased by almost 30 percent during that time, while emissions from the remaining OECD countries increased by about 70 percent, and emissions from the non-OECD nations rose by 120 percent. The declining (relative) role of the United States by no means reflects a reduction in overall vehicle emissions; rather, other economies are growing at a faster rate from a smaller base.

Vehicular fuel consumption and carbon dioxide emissions from non-OECD countries have been increasing rapidly with economic development over the past two decades. *(See Figure 12.)*

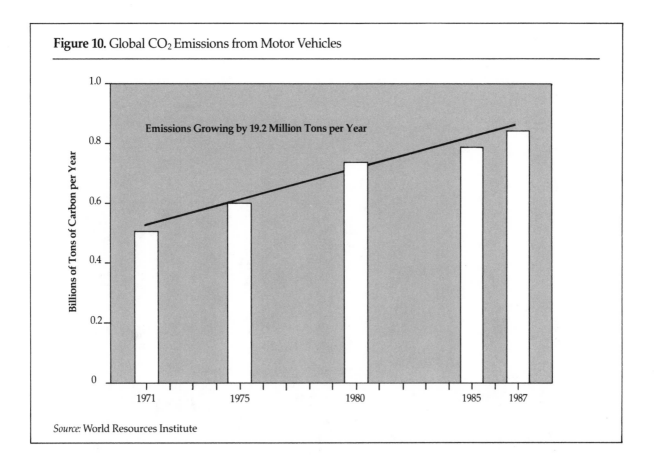

Figure 10. Global CO$_2$ Emissions from Motor Vehicles

Emissions Growing by 19.2 Million Tons per Year

Billions of Tons of Carbon per Year

Source: World Resources Institute

The nations of Eastern Europe (those that until recently had centrally planned economies) were the largest source of motor-vehicle carbon dioxide emissions outside of OECD countries in 1987, followed by Latin America, Asia, the Middle East, and Africa. Total carbon dioxide emissions from the non-OECD nations can be roughly approximated by a straight line: each year's increase equals about 8.7 million tons of carbon.

Carbon dioxide emissions from motor vehicles in the developing world are growing at about 3.5 percent per year and account for about 45 percent of the global growth in vehicle releases. As a result, emissions from developing countries—currently about 30 percent of total worldwide vehicle releases—will grow as a share of total emissions.

Carbon dioxide emissions from motor vehicles in the developing world are growing at about 3.5 percent per year and account for about 45 percent of the global growth in vehicle releases.

If worldwide growth in carbon dioxide emissions continues at its current pace, efforts to control global climate change will prove increasingly difficult. Indeed, if today's trend in carbon dioxide emissions continues, motor vehicle emissions will increase by 50 percent by the year 2010, to about 1.3 billion tons of

19

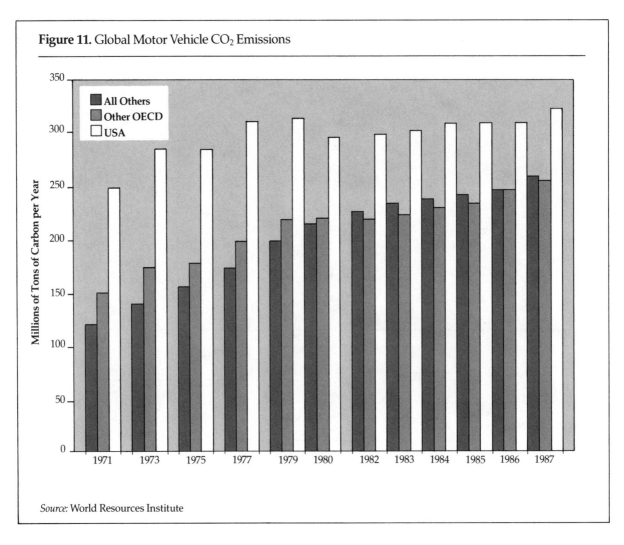

Figure 11. Global Motor Vehicle CO_2 Emissions

Millions of Tons of Carbon per Year

Legend:
- All Others
- Other OECD
- USA

Source: World Resources Institute

carbon. Avoiding such an increase will require either dampening the growth in motor vehicle emissions by improving fuel efficiency and reducing vehicle use, switching to fundamentally different transportation fuels, or both.

Along with the normal forces of economic growth are new political developments that make increases in carbon dioxide emissions more likely. With the fundamental economic reforms now taking place in Eastern Europe, industrial modernization and economic growth could lead to significant additional carbon dioxide increases. As Figure 13 shows, per-capita motor-vehicle oil consumption in the countries of Eastern Europe has averaged less than half

of that of Western Europe for the past 15 years. If Eastern Europe's per capita transportation emissions were as great today as those of Western Europe, global carbon dioxide emissions would be about 90 million tons per year greater—an amount equivalent to about half of all U.S. auto emissions.

International Programs to Improve Motor Vehicle Fuel Efficiency

How much vehicular emissions of carbon dioxide can be expected to grow depends partly on how much is done internationally to improve fuel efficiency in new vehicles. So far,

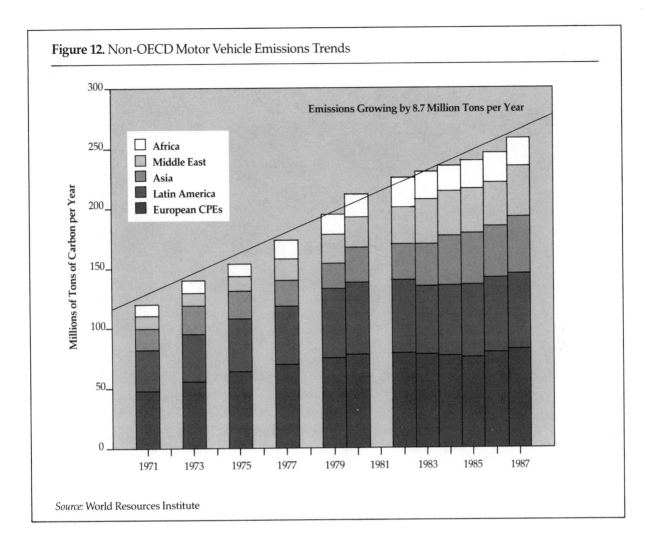

Figure 12. Non-OECD Motor Vehicle Emissions Trends

Emissions Growing by 8.7 Million Tons per Year

Millions of Tons of Carbon per Year

- Africa
- Middle East
- Asia
- Latin America
- European CPEs

Source: World Resources Institute

the amount of effort governments have devoted to improving vehicle fuel efficiency has varied widely throughout the world.

The United States has had a mandatory fuel efficiency program since 1975. The Energy Policy and Conservation Act, passed that year to come into effect in model year 1978, amended the Motor Vehicle Information and Cost Saving Act to require new passenger cars to get at least 27.5 miles per U.S. gallon (8.55 liters/100 km) by 1985, as measured by EPA test procedures.* *(See Table 5.)*

Figure 14 shows the federally mandated fuel efficiency standards for new cars in the United States, the new-car fleet fuel efficiency achieved in that year (EPA values), and the average fuel efficiency for the entire U.S. automobile fleet. (Backsliding occurred in model years 1986, 1987, and 1988 under the Reagan administration; for model year 1989, the Bush administration tightened them slightly again.)

---

*Fuel efficiencies in this report are presented in either American units of miles per U.S. gallon of fuel (mpg) or in metric units of liters per 100 kilometers (l/100 km). The conversion between these units is as follows. A vehicle with an efficiency of X mpg has a corresponding metric fuel economy of (235.3/X) liters per 100 kilometers.

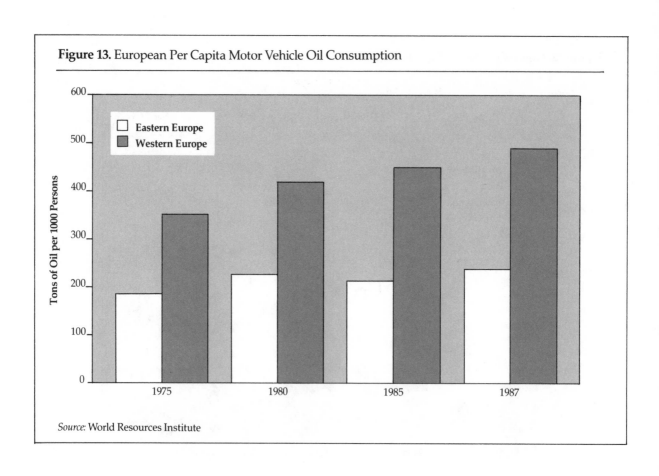

Figure 13. European Per Capita Motor Vehicle Oil Consumption

Source: World Resources Institute

Table 5. U.S. New-Car Fuel Efficiency Standards (CAFE)
(Miles per U.S. Gallon)

Model Year	Passenger Cars	Light Trucks 2 WD	Light Trucks 4 WD	Model Year	Passenger Cars	Light Trucks 2 WD	Light Trucks 4 WD
1978	18.0	—	—	1985	27.5	19.7	18.9
1979	19.0	17.2	15.8	1986	26.0	20.5	19.5
1980	20.0	16.0	14.0	1987	26.0	21.0	19.5
1981	22.0	16.7	15.0	1988	26.0	21.0	19.5
1982	24.0	18.0	16.0	1989	26.5	21.5	19.0
1983	26.0	19.5	17.5	1990	27.5	20.5	19.0
1984	27.0	20.3	18.5	1991	27.5	20.7	19.1

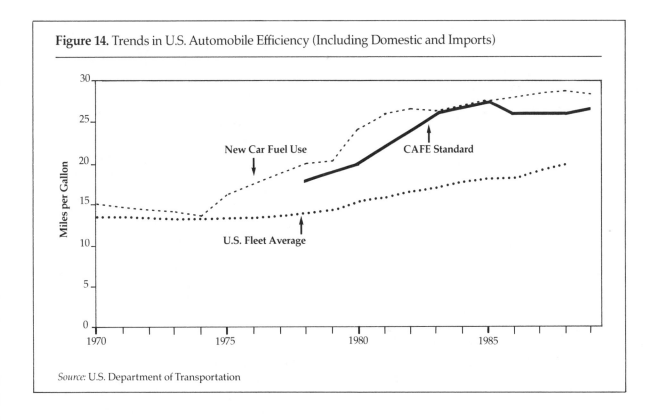

Figure 14. Trends in U.S. Automobile Efficiency (Including Domestic and Imports)

New Car Fuel Use

CAFE Standard

U.S. Fleet Average

Miles per Gallon

1970   1975   1980   1985

Source: U.S. Department of Transportation

While new-car efficiency—as measured by EPA—has increased to about 28 mpg, doubling between 1974 and 1988, the on-road fuel efficiency of the entire auto fleet has risen by only 50 percent, to about 20 mpg.[35] Moreover, for several reasons, the EPA-measured fuel efficiency of 28 mpg corresponds to a real-world value of only about 24 mpg, a 15-percent difference: Highway driving speeds are greater than those assumed by EPA and automobiles are less efficient at high speeds; the fraction of miles driven in cities (where fuel efficiencies are generally less) is greater than assumed in the federal test procedures;[36] and urban areas are becoming increasingly congested reducing fuel efficiencies even further. Total fuel consumption for the United States is also higher because light trucks and minivans are increasingly being used in place of automobiles. At any rate, the average fuel efficiency for the entire passenger-car fleet should plateau at about 24 mpg (9.8 l/100 km) unless new-car efficiency improves.

Significantly, U.S. efficiency improvements began with the industrialized world's least-efficient car fleet.[37] Only after the dramatic improvements observed to date are typical U.S. cars generally as efficient as those in the same weight class in other countries.

In recent years, as fuel prices have dropped and the CAFE pressures to improve fuel efficiency have diminished, U.S. new-car fuel efficiency has begun to slip. According to EPA, the fuel efficiency of new U.S. cars declined 4 percent between 1988 and 1990.[38] Domestic vehicles declined 3 percent while Asian models (from Japan and Korea) declined 6 percent. Over this same period, the new-car fleet (domestic and imports) showed a 6-percent weight gain and a 10-percent increase in horsepower. According to EPA, "if this backslide continues, problems with nationwide fuel consumption will increase and global warming trends will worsen at a pace faster than is generally being assumed by analysts."

EPA data suggest that the fuel efficiency wars of the late 1970s gave way to horsepower wars in the 1980s. Throughout the decade, manufacturers substantially increased cars' power output. Unfortunately, in the real world, drivers with more horsepower available tend to accelerate their vehicles faster, thus using more fuel and needlessly increasing on-road emissions of nitrogen oxides, volatile organic compounds, and carbon monoxide.

Compounding the problem of smaller efficiency gains in new cars has been the already-noted switch by many drivers from automobiles to light-duty trucks, which aren't as fuel-efficient as cars. In 1988, U.S. retail sales of light-duty trucks (those weighing less than 6000 pounds) totalled 3.5 million, fully a third of the number of automobiles sold.[39] Most people use these vehicles much like passenger cars—unfortunate since new domestically manufactured trucks average only 20 mpg and imports 24 mpg, compared with 28 mpg for new cars.[40]

More and more commuters are switching from autos and public transit to trucks. In 1969, only 8 percent of commuting trips were in trucks; in 1983, some 15 percent were.[41] Similarly, in 1969 public transportation was used for 8.4 percent of trips to work while in 1983 the figure was only 5.8 percent.[42] About 83 percent of commuters used cars to get to work in 1969 while only 78 percent did in 1983.

Apparently, low fuel prices can offset many of the gains resulting from federal CAFE standards.

There is little doubt that the rise in sales of trucks and big cars and the decline in U.S. motor-vehicle fuel efficiency both stem largely from the substantial drop in real fuel prices

Vehicle manufacturers are required to test some percentage of all vehicles destined to be sold in the United States so that a fuel-consumption rating can be assigned to each product line. The test involves both city and highway driving cycles. From these figures, a sales-weighted average fuel-consumption figure is calculated for all the passenger cars produced by each manufacturer. Fuel efficiency (in mpg) calculated this way must exceed the Corporate Average Fuel Economy (CAFE) standard specified for the appropriate model year. Since the 1979 model year, the CAFE program, as it is called, has been expanded to cover light-duty trucks as well as passenger cars.

Failure to meet the CAFE requirements can result in substantial financial penalties. For each vehicle produced, a manufacturer whose fleet-average fuel consumption does not meet the CAFE standard is fined $5 per vehicle for every 0.1 miles/U.S. gallon by which the standard is not met. These fines may be offset by credits accrued in other model years, however. In 1990, GM, Ford, and Chrysler all failed to meet the 27.5 mpg standard. Since 1983, the federal government has collected $164 million in CAFE fines.

since the mid-1980s. As Figure 15 shows, gasoline prices (expressed in constant 1989 dollars) were about as low in 1989 as they had been in the previous 39 years. Apparently, low fuel prices can offset many of the gains resulting from the federal CAFE standards that require manufacturers to produce lighter and more efficient vehicles.

People who buy especially inefficient new cars do pay some financial penalties for the privilege. "Gas guzzler" taxes are levied on vehicles that do not achieve certain minimum fuel economy figures. *(See Table 6.)* In 1986, the

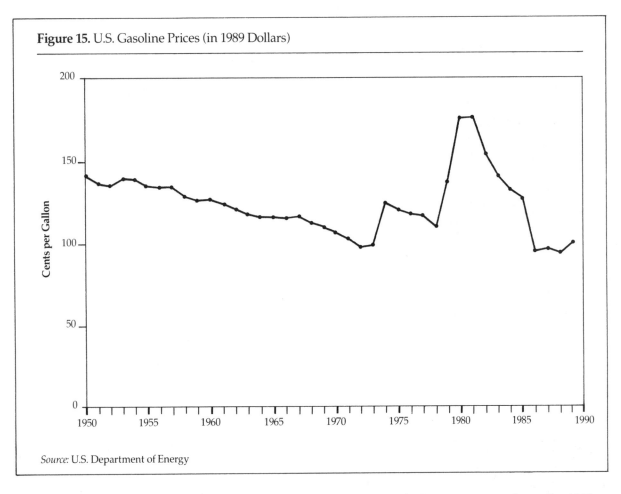

Figure 15. U.S. Gasoline Prices (in 1989 Dollars)

Cents per Gallon

Source: U.S. Department of Energy

tax ranged from $500 for a 0.1 mile/U.S. gallon shortfall to a maximum of $3,850.

Table 6. Minimum Fuel Efficiencies for Gas Guzzler Taxes

1984	19.5 miles/U.S. gal	(12.1 l/100 km)
1985	21.0　　''	(11.2　'' 　)
1986 and after.	22.5　　''	(10.5　'' 　)

Compared to the United States, Europe has relied more on higher fuel prices, consumer information, and voluntary programs to encourage improved transportation efficiency. In France and the United Kingdom, fuel-efficiency programs are limited to mandatory publication of vehicular fuel consumption data. *(See Table 7.)* But in several other countries (among them Sweden and Australia), major manufacturers have voluntarily improved vehicle fuel efficiency. Some countries have also reduced speed limits and imposed higher taxes on gas guzzlers to reduce fuel consumption.

While no European country has so far made improvements in fuel efficiency mandatory, car manufacturers in several countries have voluntarily agreed to reduce new-car fuel use by around 10 percent. Sweden has specified fuel-efficiency standards, averaged over all cars produced in a given year, which each manufacturer is expected to meet.

The Japanese government has made improvements in fuel consumption of passenger cars

25

Besides the CAFE requirements, the federal program also provides consumers with information about the relative efficiency of new cars. The 'Gas Mileage Guide' published by EPA and the Department of Energy lists the city and highway fuel consumption test results of each vehicle model and is intended to provide information to new-car buyers. Also required on new cars are stickers indicating the vehicle fuel consumption as determined by EPA, an estimate of the annual fuel cost based on 15,000 miles of operation, and the range of fuel economy achieved by similar sized vehicles of other makes. The mpg estimates on these stickers have been adjusted by EPA to give a somewhat more realistic estimate of the on-the-road fuel consumption that the owner can expect under average driving conditions and to allow a comparison between different vehicle models.

mandatory. According to law, new-car efficiency improvements of between 6 and 11 percent, relative to 1978, had to be achieved by 1985. *(See Table 8.)* Standards have been specified by vehicle weight, and efficiency is measured using a 10-mode test procedure. However, with the increased worldwide availability of low-cost oil in the late 1980s, average new-vehicle fuel economy in Japan started to slip: in 1988, it averaged only 27.3 mpg, compared with 30.5 mpg in 1982.

In Australia, the trend toward improved fuel efficiency has been largely the result of voluntary efforts by the auto industry. In response to a federal report on energy conservation, the Federal Chamber of Automotive Industries (FCAI) proposed a voluntary "Code of Practice for Passenger Car Fuel Consumption Reduction." Under this code, FCAI set annual goals for National Average Fuel Consumption (NAFC); with these goals in mind, a sales-weighted Corporate Average Fuel Consumption (CAFC) target for new cars was derived for each manufacturer. The base level NAFC

Table 7. European Agreements for Reductions in New-Vehicle Fuel Consumption

Country	Requirements
U.K.	Compulsory reporting of fuel consumption data. Ten percent increase in mpg (9.1 percent reduction in fuel consumption) from 1978 levels, by 1985, for passenger cars only (diesels excluded).
France	Compulsory reporting of fuel consumption data. Mean fuel consumption in new automobiles to be less than 7.5 liters/100 km (greater than 31 mpg) by 1985.
West Germany	Ten to twenty percent reduction (5 percent for heavy trucks) in fuel consumption in new autos, relative to 1978, by 1985. The target of 12 percent for new cars has already been achieved. The German auto industry was expected to achieve 15 percent.
Italy	Ten percent lower consumption in new autos, from 1978 levels, by 1985.
Sweden	New-Car Fleet averages: 8.5 l/100 km (28 mpg) by 1985 7.5 l/100 km (31 mpg) by 1990 Voluntary, but will be made mandatory in the event of noncompliance.

Table 8. Japanese New-Car Fuel Efficiency Standards
Units: liters/100 km and (mpg)

	Inertia Weight Category, (kg)			
	625	**750–875**	**1000–1250**	**1500–2000**
1978 Actual fuel consumption	5.38 (44 mpg)	6.94 (34)	9.01 (26)	13.16 (18)
1985 Legislated fuel consumption	5.05 (46)	6.25 (38)	8.00 (29)	11.76 (20)
Improvement %	6.1	9.9	11.2	10.6

for 1978 was 11.2 liters/100 km (21 mpg), and the FCAI goal for 1983 was 9.0 liters/100 km (26 mpg). The Australian auto industry has acknowledged that a further improvement to 8 liters/100 km (29 mpg) is feasible.

Even without regulatory programs like those of the United States, Europeans and Japanese consume far less motor fuel per person than Americans do, partly because fuel taxes and fees on motor vehicles themselves are higher, and partly because more public-transportation options are available. In Japan and most European countries, motor fuels cost drivers at least twice what they do in the United States; in a number of countries, they are more than four times as expensive. With fuels so heavily taxed, it should come as no surprise that corresponding per capita use in these countries is less than half that of the United States. (See Figure 16.) Per capita motor vehicle travel in these countries is also less than half of what it is in the United States.[43]

As this brief summary shows, over the past few years the fuel-economy gains made in the 1970s and early 1980s in many countries has begun to erode. Most of the programs that made these savings possible have now stalled. In the United States, low fuel prices combined with a failure to strengthen federal fuel efficiency (CAFE) standards have led to recent declines in new-car fuel efficiency, a trend with ominous implications for the nation's overall carbon dioxide emissions.

Future Trends in Global Motor Vehicle Production, Registrations, and Carbon Dioxide Emissions

Worldwide, the number of motor vehicles is growing far faster than the global population—4.6 percent per year between 1975 and 1980, compared with 1.74 percent per year. The same holds even in the United States, which already has by far the world's highest per capita vehicle population. (See Figure 9.) According to recently reported projections (1990) by DRI, Inc.,[44] global auto production in western countries will continue growing over the next five years. (See Figure 17.) By 1995, auto production in Western Europe, North America, Asia, and Latin America is expected to increase by 16 percent over 1988 values. Truck production in North America and Western Europe combined is also projected to grow by 16 percent.

The size of the global fleet will also grow. According to DRI, Inc., global new-car registrations are projected to rise by 16 percent between 1988 and 1995.[45] The largest increases in vehicle use are expected in regions that now have the fewest vehicles per capita—the Asia-Pacific region (96 percent, excluding Japan), Africa and the Middle East (40 percent), the

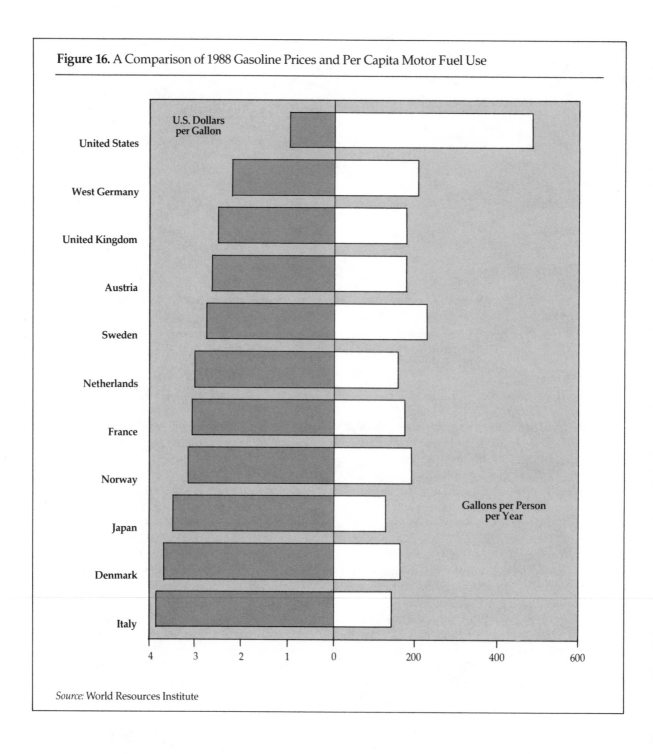

Figure 16. A Comparison of 1988 Gasoline Prices and Per Capita Motor Fuel Use

U.S. Dollars
per Gallon

United States

West Germany

United Kingdom

Austria

Sweden

Netherlands

France

Norway

Gallons per Person
per Year

Japan

Denmark

Italy

4   3   2   1   0   200   400   600

Source: World Resources Institute

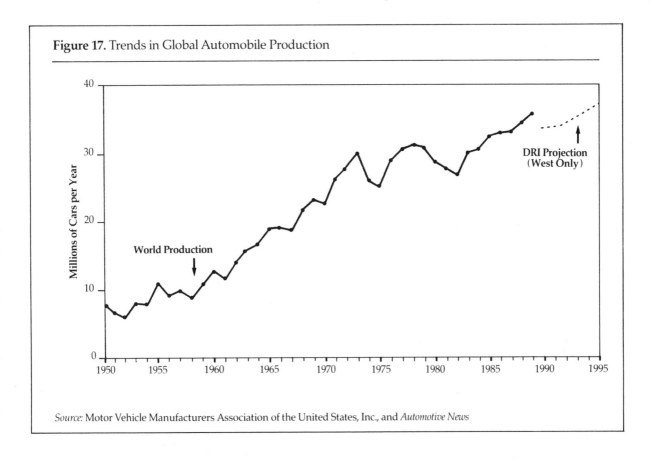

Figure 17. Trends in Global Automobile Production

Millions of Cars per Year

World Production

DRI Projection
(West Only)

Source: Motor Vehicle Manufacturers Association of the United States, Inc., and *Automotive News*

eastern bloc (31 percent), and Latin America (17 percent). Still, rapid new-vehicle growth won't occur everywhere. New-car registrations are expected to grow by only 12 percent in Western Europe and to hold steady at today's levels in the United States.

One way to estimate future global motor-vehicle registrations is to analyze recent trends in the growth of the global fleet. Another is to analyze trends in per capita motor vehicle registrations and population growth. Of course, both are subject to considerable uncertainty related to political upheavals such as Iraq's invasion of Kuwait, and to economic variables such as trends in the price and availability of oil. Still, despite several wars, economic recessions, and two major global energy shocks, growth in vehicle use has continued unabated over the past 40 years.

Analyzing trends in global motor vehicle registrations reveals that the global fleet has been growing linearly since just before 1970 and that each year for two decades an additional 16 million motor vehicles have been added to the world fleet. As Figure 18 shows, if this linear trend continues, the global vehicle population will reach about 885 million by the year 2010—an increase of over 70 percent since 1987. By the year 2025, there would be over 1.1 billion vehicles, a figure consistent with the projections made by individual countries.[46]

Analyzing growth in registrations per capita yields what is probably an upper bound for the world motor vehicle fleet. As Figure 19 shows, each year worldwide registrations grow by about 2 vehicles per thousand persons. If this trend were to continue until 2010, there would be 154 motor vehicles per 1000 persons,

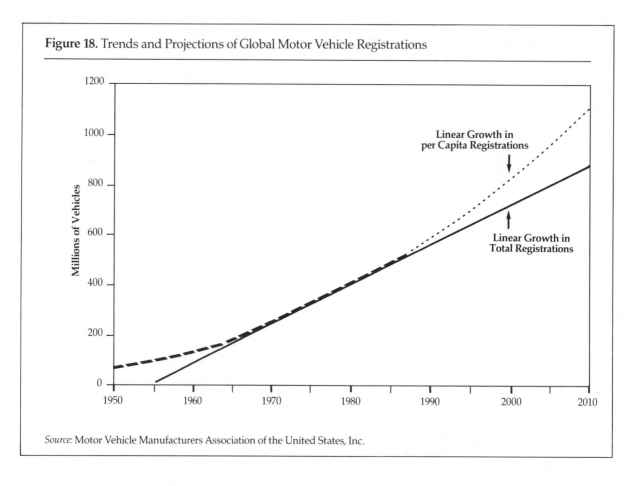

Figure 18. Trends and Projections of Global Motor Vehicle Registrations

Source: Motor Vehicle Manufacturers Association of the United States, Inc.

compared with 112 in 1990. If this figure is multiplied by the United Nation's[47] medium variant estimate for global population in 2010—7.2 billion—the motor vehicle fleet turns out to be an estimated 1.1 billion, which is 115 percent higher than in 1987. This number is about 25 percent greater than the strictly linear projection of growth in total registrations (885 million). *(See Figure 18.)*

A plausible range for carbon dioxide emissions from the global motor vehicle fleet can be calculated by examining recent emission trends. (Total emissions depend on the size of the global fleet, the vehicles' average fuel efficiency, the number of miles driven annually, and the type of fuel burned.) As Figure 20 shows, total carbon dioxide emissions *per vehicle* declined between 1970 and 1987 by about 20 percent—a decline that closely follows the

exponential curve depicted as a solid line in the figure. On average, individual motor-vehicle carbon emissions fell by 1.5 percent annually between 1970 and 1987 for the entire global fleet (both old vehicles and new). The decline seen in Figure 20 reflects not only improvements that have occurred in new-vehicle fuel efficiency, but also increased congestion, higher average vehicle speeds, and an increase in the number of vehicle miles traveled.

Will this worldwide trend toward declining carbon dioxide emissions per vehicle continue? Obviously, there is no way of knowing for sure, but there is troubling evidence that, worldwide, new cars are becoming less efficient. As mentioned, new-car fuel economy is dropping in Japan, Western Europe, and in several developing countries; in the United

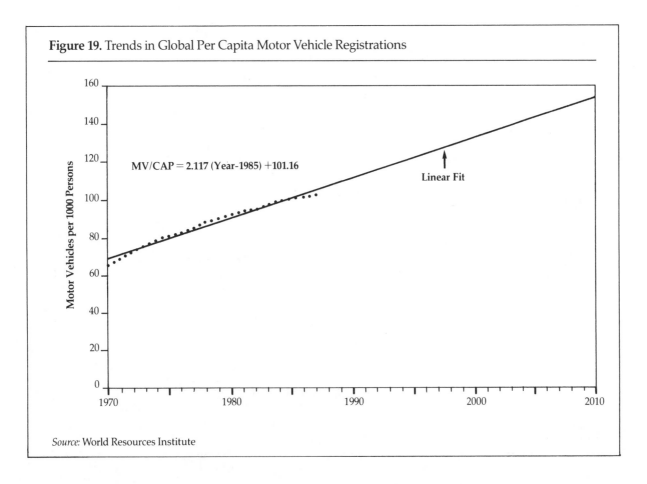

Figure 19. Trends in Global Per Capita Motor Vehicle Registrations

$$MV/CAP = 2.117 \, (Year\text{-}1985) + 101.16$$

Linear Fit

Motor Vehicles per 1000 Persons

Source: World Resources Institute

States, new-car fuel efficiency dropped 4 percent between 1988 and 1990. Meanwhile, the average number of miles traveled per motor vehicle rose by 11 percent between 1980 and 1987,[48] congestion increased, and vehicle speeds rose—all of which tend to increase the fuel used per vehicle. If these various trends continue, recent patterns toward declining fuel used per vehicle will slow, if not reverse themselves.

Such backsliding is not inevitable, however, and a continuation of the decline in carbon dioxide emissions (per vehicle) is still technologically feasible. If *new-vehicle* fuel consumption (the net result of vehicle efficiency, congestion, driving habits, etc.) were to drop by 50 percent relative to 1970 by the year 2000, then the fuel used per vehicle for the entire fleet would drop by half within the decade or

so that it takes for the fleet to turn over. Were such an improvement to occur—even in the face of increasing congestion, higher driving speeds, and so forth—the average amount of fuel used and carbon dioxide emitted per motor vehicle worldwide would fall by about half between 1970 and 2010, as Figure 20 indicates.

If the number of motor vehicles worldwide increases somewhere between the two trends indicated in Figure 18 and average carbon dioxide emissions per vehicle continue to fall as they do in Figure 20—perhaps an optimistic assumption given the countervailing trends of the past few years—then projecting the growth in global carbon dioxide emissions from vehicles is a fairly straightforward matter. At the low end, with the number of vehicles increasing linearly, carbon dioxide emissions would

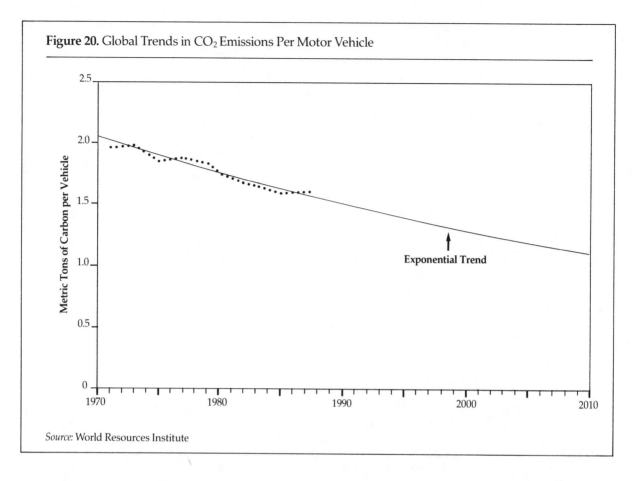

Figure 20. Global Trends in CO$_2$ Emissions Per Motor Vehicle

Metric Tons of Carbon per Vehicle

Exponential Trend

Source: World Resources Institute

grow from about 820 million tons (of carbon) in 1987 to about 980 million tons in 2010, a jump of about 20 percent. *(See Figure 21.)* At the high end—assuming that per capita motor vehicle use increases linearly and the world population grows to about 7.2 billion, as projected by the United Nations in its ''medium variant''— carbon dioxide emissions would swell to about 1.2 billion tons (of carbon) in 2010, an increase of 50 percent over 1987.

These projections of 20 to 50 percent increases in motor vehicle carbon dioxide emissions by 2010 may well be the lower bounds of future trends. Indeed, per-vehicle emissions from the global fleet won't keep declining if recent patterns of lower new-vehicle efficiency, more congestion, higher speeds, and more vehicle-miles-traveled hold. Clearly, without major international efforts to reduce future

carbon dioxide emissions, global efforts to control global climate change could be overwhelmed.

Trends in the U.S. Motor Vehicle Fleet

The trends in U.S. vehicle growth and emissions generally resemble global patterns. *(See Figures 22 through 24.)* As Figure 22 shows, the number of registered motor vehicles in the United States has grown by an average of 4 million motor vehicles annually since at least 1970. If this linear trend continues, the U.S. fleet would total about 273 million motor vehicles in the year 2010, compared with 183 million in 1988. (A fleet only slightly larger is predicted from a linear extrapolation of the trend in per capita motor vehicle registrations.)

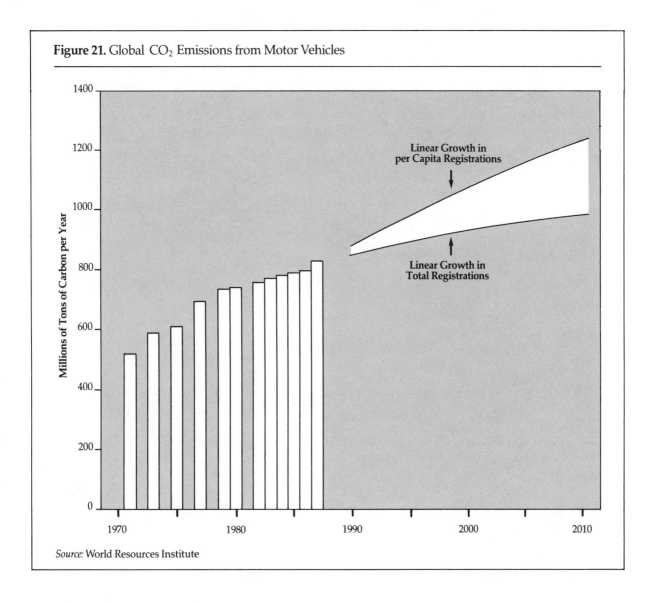

Figure 21. Global CO$_2$ Emissions from Motor Vehicles

Source: World Resources Institute

As Figure 23 shows, the U.S. motor vehicle fleet's carbon dioxide emissions (figured on a per-vehicle basis) declined by about 1.5 percent per year between 1971 and 1988. This decline reflects all the factors affecting vehicle fuel consumption, including improved new-vehicle efficiency partially offset by more congestion, more urban driving, greater highway speeds, and so forth. But data collected since 1980 suggest that the rate of fleet improvement has slowed. Most likely, a combination of factors is at work: the recent reduction in new-vehicle

fuel performance, increases in the number of miles driven per vehicle, rural driving speeds, urban driving and congestion, and the use of trucks and vans for individual commuting.

If emissions *per vehicle* continue their downward trend at 1.5 percent per year, continuing the pattern of Figure 23, carbon dioxide emissions from U.S. motor vehicles will increase by about 6 percent by the year 2010. *(See Figure 24.)* If, instead, the countertrends just mentioned prevail and carbon dioxide emissions

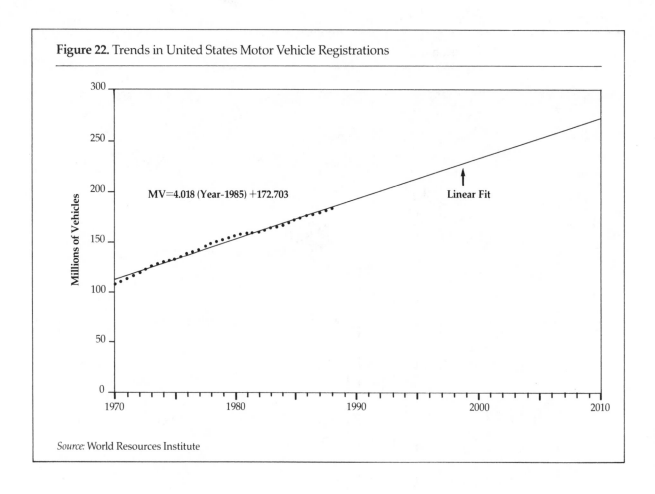

Figure 22. Trends in United States Motor Vehicle Registrations

$$MV = 4.018\,(\text{Year}-1985) + 172.703$$

Linear Fit

Source: World Resources Institute

per vehicle don't fall below the 1985–1988 average through the year 2010, emissions will increase by 50 percent: from 329 million tons of carbon in 1988 to about 496 million tons in the year 2010.

Can the growth in carbon dioxide emissions from U.S. motor vehicles be contained, or even reversed? Fortunately, the answer is yes, and there are undoubtedly various combinations of policies that would achieve this important goal. Indeed, any serious national effort to cut carbon dioxide emissions must integrate several options—chief among them, improved new-vehicle efficiency, better traffic management, enforcement of speed limits, car and van pooling, better vehicle maintenance, improved driving habits, and the use of non-fossil fuels.

Any serious national effort to cut carbon dioxide emissions must integrate several options—chief among them, improved new-vehicle efficiency, better traffic management, enforcement of speed limits, car and van pooling, better vehicle maintenance, improved driving habits, and the use of non-fossil fuels.

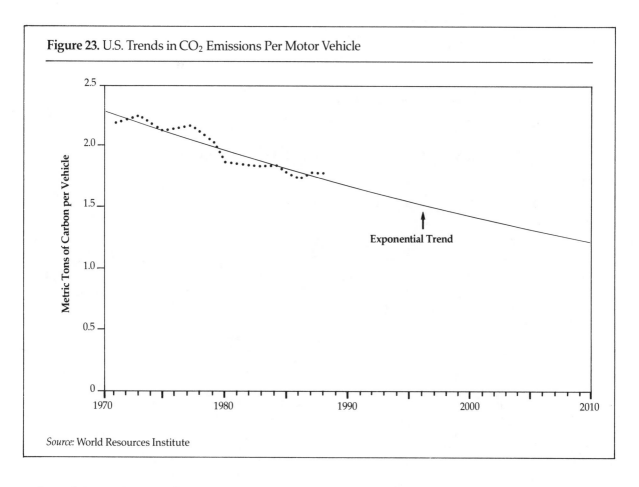

Figure 23. U.S. Trends in CO_2 Emissions Per Motor Vehicle

Metric Tons of Carbon per Vehicle

Exponential Trend

Source: World Resources Institute

Consider just the potential impacts for improving new-car fuel efficiency. Figure 25 shows the trend in on-the-road fuel efficiency among new cars in the United States between 1970 and 1987, along with four possible future paths beginning in 1987: no improvement over today's 24 mpg average; and improvement rates of 1 percent, 2 percent, and 3 percent per year in new-car fuel efficiency. (The more recent fuel efficiency values in Figure 25 have been adjusted downward by 15 percent from those reported by EPA to reflect the differences between EPA's test procedures and on-the-road experiences.) The fuel efficiencies reached by the year 2010 are given in Table 9 along with approximate values corresponding to the EPA test procedures. (A 30-percent difference between "EPA" and "on-the-road" values has been assumed for the year 2010[49] to account for the effects of urban congestion, more urban

Table 9. New-Car Fuel Efficiencies in 2010 ("On-the-Road" and "EPA-Equivalent") Resulting from Four Different Assumed Growth Rates

Compound Growth Rate	On-the-Road	EPA Fuel Efficiency
0%	24 mpg	34 mpg
1%	30 mpg	43 mpg
2%	38 mpg	54 mpg
3%	47 mpg	67 mpg

driving, and so forth on fuel use.) As Table 9 shows, if the fuel efficiency of new cars increased by 2 percent per year, on-the-road mileage for new cars would reach about 38 mpg in the year 2010, corresponding to an

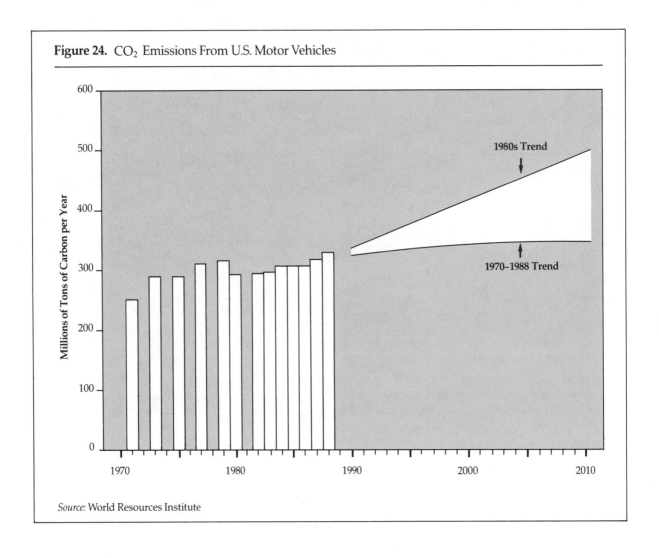

Figure 24. CO$_2$ Emissions From U.S. Motor Vehicles

Source: World Resources Institute

EPA-measured fuel efficiency of about 54 mpg. If annual improvements of 3 percent were achieved, on-the-road efficiency would reach 47 mpg, corresponding to an EPA rating of about 67 mpg.

Where do these four different paths lead in terms of carbon dioxide emissions? If automobile-miles-traveled continue growing by 27 billion per year and the fuel efficiency of new cars doesn't improve further, by the year 2010 carbon dioxide emissions from the total U.S. auto fleet would increase by more than 20

percent relative to late 1980 emission levels. *(See Figure 26.)* If the fuel efficiency of new cars increased by 1 percent per year, corresponding to an EPA fuel efficiency of about 43 mpg by 2010, carbon dioxide emissions would increase by a few percentage points relative to the late 1980s. A 2-percent per year improvement, which would bring new-car efficiency to about 54 mpg (measured by EPA test procedures) by 2010, would start reducing carbon dioxide emissions almost immediately. A 3-percent improvement—corresponding to a new-car efficiency of 67 mpg by 2010—would cut carbon

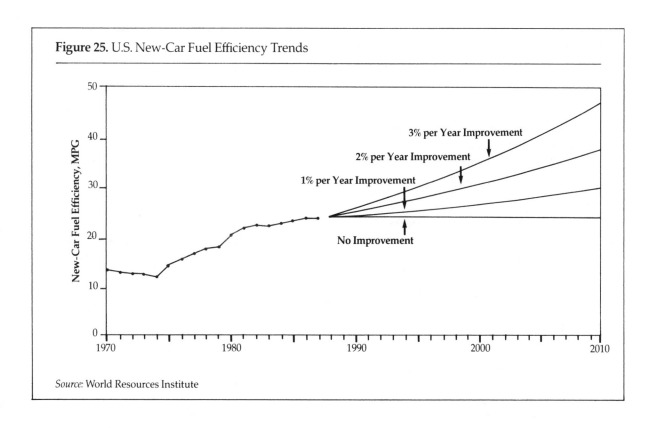

Figure 25. U.S. New-Car Fuel Efficiency Trends

3% per Year Improvement

2% per Year Improvement

1% per Year Improvement

No Improvement

New-Car Fuel Efficiency, MPG

Source: World Resources Institute

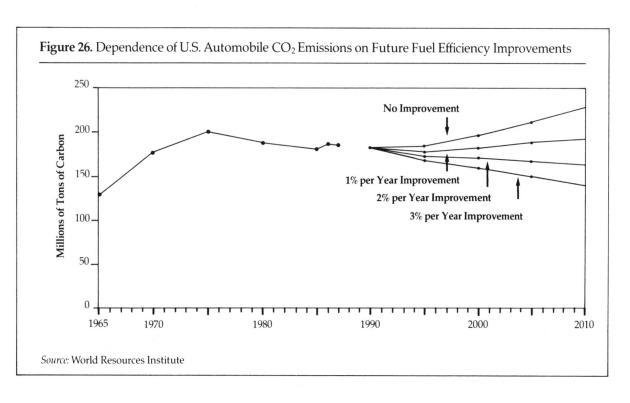

Figure 26. Dependence of U.S. Automobile CO_2 Emissions on Future Fuel Efficiency Improvements

No Improvement

1% per Year Improvement

2% per Year Improvement

3% per Year Improvement

Millions of Tons of Carbon

Source: World Resources Institute

dioxide emissions by about one fourth by 2010.** Comparable improvements in other vehicle categories—light and heavy trucks and buses—are also needed to bring about comparable reductions in carbon dioxide emissions.

These calculations illustrate the difficulty of relying *solely* on technological improvements in new vehicles to reduce carbon emissions: increasingly large improvements in the fuel efficiency of new vehicles would be needed to make such a strategy work. And such improvements would have to continue indefinitely if growth in vehicle use continues. Indeed, this conclusion is reinforced by experience over the past fifteen years with passenger-car fuel efficiency in the United States: despite a major successful effort to double new-car fuel efficiency between 1974 and 1988, and a 30-percent fleet-wide reduction in gasoline consumption per automobile, total automobile gasoline consumption was still 6 percent higher in 1988 than in 1970. Total U.S. fuel consumption by cars, trucks, and buses actually grew by about 40 percent during this period.[50]

Internationally, efficiency gains have also been overwhelmed by the number of miles driven. Between 1973 and 1987, the average quantity of fuel consumed per vehicle in the global motor fleet decreased by about 20 percent. Yet, total fuel consumption rose by about 40 percent, paced by a 70-percent rise in the number of vehicles.

The inescapable conclusion is that improvements in new-vehicle fuel efficiency—as

Improvements in new-vehicle fuel efficiency—as necessary as they are—will not by themselves significantly reduce carbon dioxide emissions from the transport sector if growth in overall motor-vehicle use continues along present lines.

necessary as they are—will not by themselves significantly reduce carbon dioxide emissions from the transport sector if growth in overall motor-vehicle use continues along present lines. A successful emissions-reduction strategy will also have to be grounded in overall efficiency improvements in transportation systems and, in the longer term, fundamental changes in the energy sources used in transportation. A broad spectrum of measures is needed to reduce emissions. These include reducing congestion, keeping highway speeds down, increasing capacity factors in all types of vehicles, and slowing the growth in vehicle miles traveled.

**Although large improvements become increasingly difficult to achieve, new-car fuel efficiency (as measured by EPA) did grow by more than 7 percent per year between 1974 and 1984, doubling from 13 mpg to almost 27 mpg.

V. Summary, Analysis, and Policy Recommendations

The challenge of controlling greenhouse warming is truly daunting, and reducing carbon dioxide emissions—an important part of that strategy—will eventually require profound changes in global patterns of energy supply and use. According to EPA estimates, simply stabilizing atmospheric concentrations of carbon dioxide at existing levels will require reducing anthropogenic carbon dioxide emissions by 50 to 85 percent below current values.[51]

Motor vehicles, major direct and indirect sources of greenhouse gases, account for about 14 percent of global fuel-related carbon dioxide emissions, and these emissions are growing by about 2.4 percent per year. Just to stabilize, much less reduce, these emissions will tax our creativity and resources, and part of any strategy to control carbon dioxide emissions must be greatly improving new-vehicle fuel efficiency. Still, by itself, improved efficiency can't get the job done if motor vehicle use continues to grow. Indeed, the very real benefits from such improvements will eventually be canceled out by the impacts of more vehicles being driven more miles.

The four broad policy recommendations offered below would provide the foundations for a long-term transportation policy for the United States while gradually reducing the threats from petroleum-powered vehicles to the climate and air quality. Obviously, what the United States does as the world's largest source of transportation-related carbon dioxide emissions will influence other nations both developing and industrialized. Many measures taken here are also highly applicable to other countries' transportation systems.

1. Further Improving New-Vehicle Fuel Efficiency

The analysis presented here suggests that over the next two decades headway could be made in bringing carbon dioxide emissions from transportation under control by accelerating the global trend toward fewer carbon dioxide emissions per vehicle. Moreover, experience gained during the 1970s and 1980s in the United States and Europe suggests that the dual goals of improved fuel efficiency (and therefore lower carbon dioxide emissions) and lowered pollution emissions are complementary rather than antagonistic. As a result, air pollution emissions could also be reduced at the same time.

The dual goals of improved fuel efficiency (and therefore lower carbon dioxide emissions) and lowered pollution emissions are complementary rather than antagonistic.

Despite the recent countertrends in the production of more fuel-efficient vehicles, major improvements in on-the-road new-vehicle efficiency are possible over the next 15 to 20 years using technology that is now market-ready or nearly so.[52] So-called "concept" vehicles employing much of this advanced technology already exist.[53] In 1985, the Toyota Corporation tested a light-weight prototype car, dubbed the AXV (for Advanced Experimental Vehicle), that features low aerodynamic drag, a direct-injection diesel engine, a continuously variable transmission, and other well understood design features. The car received an EPA fuel economy rating of 98 miles per gallon on the combined urban/highway test. Similarly, the Volvo LCP 2000 (for Light Component Project), also dating from 1985, gets 65 mpg in mixed driving and up to 100 mpg at a constant 40 mph. This Volvo, powered by a 3-cylinder direct-injected diesel engine, can accelerate to over 60 mph in 11 seconds. While these vehicles are not yet being considered for commercial production and may not meet all current U.S. safety and emission requirements, they do demonstrate the feasibility of increasing fuel efficiencies by adopting new technologies.

To help get more highly efficient vehicles on the road, especially to substitute for older, less-efficient, more polluting vehicles, an international working group of major vehicle-producing countries is needed. Logistically, this group should be easy enough to organize since only fourteen manufacturers produce 80 percent of the world's motor vehicles and are all based in the United States, Japan, West Germany, France, and Italy. Composed of manufacturers and various international government representatives, the working group would address these issues with the ultimate goal of adopting international targets for improved vehicle efficiency that producers worldwide would agree to meet.

These efficiency targets should be supplemented by international efforts by the United States, the nations of Western Europe, and Japan, and other countries with large numbers of vehicles to create markets for highly efficient cars, trucks, and buses. Without question, the United States could create such markets and encourage efficiency improvements by adopting measures such as gas-guzzler/gas-sipper taxes on new vehicles, annual registration fees on all motor vehicles graduated according to fuel efficiency, mandatory fuel efficiency standards, and carbon taxes on fossil fuels.

A broad-based carbon tax on fossil fuels—already under consideration by several European countries—is an especially attractive means of encouraging efficiency because it would begin to make *all* fossil fuel prices reflect the climate risks and other environmental costs associated with each fuel. A carbon tax would be relatively easy to administer federally and could be adjusted upward or downward as more information on climate becomes available. Such a tax would encourage fuel users in all sectors of the economy, not just commuters and other drivers, to use energy more efficiently. It would also encourage the development and use of non-fossil energy sources, and the funds raised this way could be used to mitigate the impacts of global warming.

2. Increasing Transportation System Efficiency

Additional reductions in vehicular emissions of carbon dioxide (as well as noxious air pollutants) can be achieved by reducing dependence on individual cars and trucks and by making greater use of van and car pools, buses, trolleys, and trains. Improving urban traffic management by installing synchronized traffic lights, reducing on-street parking, switching to "smart" roads, banning truck unloading during the day, and so forth can also improve transportation system fuel efficiency.[54]

Providing efficient, convenient, and affordable public transportation alternatives worldwide would produce multiple benefits. For every 40 persons who get out of their cars and onto a bus for a ten-mile-trip to work, some 50 to 75 pounds of carbon are not emitted to the air. Greater use of public transportation would reduce congestion, cut fatalities and injuries from traffic accidents, and greatly improve air quality. Fortunately, such transportation improvements can be phased in over time. For example, roadways initially dedicated to bus traffic can later be upgraded to light rail or heavy rail if circumstances warrant.

The financial and institutional barriers to introducing efficient public transportation systems—especially light- and heavy-rail—can be formidable. However, though rail systems are expensive to construct and sometimes disruptive to install, (particularly in large metropolitan areas), over the long term they still make sense for many densely populated areas.

Since no two cities are laid out the same or have identical transportation infrastructures, few categorical rules can be given for improving transportation system efficiency. What is clear, however, is that in the United States, transportation planning is best accomplished regionally with active community participation. The problems are best understood at this level and the chances of balanced planning are greatest. Perhaps the most important federal contribution would be to provide adequate financial assistance to regional planning organizations to support open transportation planning with active community participation and to make financial assistance available on an equal footing for all options to implement regionally developed transportation programs.

3. Developing Non-Fossil Energy Sources for Transportation

While technological improvements in petroleum-powered vehicles are essential to achieving short-term increases in the vehicle fleet's fuel efficiency, they will not—as this analysis makes clear—be sufficient for the long haul if the global vehicle fleet continues growing. For this reason, longer-term international efforts to develop new transportation energy sources that emit no carbon dioxide will have to be intensified as emissions are reduced. A program of research, development, demonstration, and,

ultimately, the introduction of such vehicles should become a matter of high public priority, not just for the United States but for all the principal vehicle-producing nations.

The two energy sources that are most attractive today to power the cars and trucks of tomorrow are electricity and hydrogen. Renewable technologies—such as hydroelectric plants, wind turbines, solar electric power plants, photovoltaic cells, ocean-wave power plants, and geothermal plants—are potential electricity sources that emit no carbon dioxide. As for hydrogen, it can be obtained with electricity from water through electrolysis or, directly, through photoelectrochemical decomposition.

The principal obstacle to the widespread introduction of electric or hydrogen-powered vehicles is not so much the availability or cost of electricity from solar or other non-fossil energy sources. Rather, the obstacle is technical: providing adequate energy storage on board the vehicle itself.

Electric vehicles have traditionally been powered by lead-acid batteries, which are heavy and relatively short lived. Improved batteries with higher energy densities (such as the nickel-iron battery) look promising. Also attractive for use in electric vehicles are "ultracapacitors"—electricity-storage devices now under development that promise to boost acceleration, double the range of today's electric vehicles, and extend battery life.[55] Eventually, ultracapacitors could eliminate the need for batteries altogether.

The high cost of batteries and the short range of electric vehicles might also be addressed through nationwide battery-leasing programs. Under such programs, consumers would pay a national supplier a monthly usage fee. They could recharge their vehicles at night at home or, for an additional charge, drive into a battery station operated by the leasing company when the batteries were low and have them replaced with a fully charged replacement unit in a few minutes.

The Los Angeles Department of Water and Power, along with Southern California Edison, have ordered 10,000 hybrid electric vehicles to be on the road by 1995. These vehicles will be equipped with batteries that will power them for about 60 miles and gasoline engines to charge the batteries for longer trips. The California Air Resources Board has also adopted regulations that will require that 10 percent of all new vehicles have zero emissions by the year 2003, a condition that can currently be met only by electric vehicles.

U.S. automakers are also showing a serious intent to introduce electric vehicles. General Motors has developed a prototype high-performance two-passenger electric car (the Impact) that has a range of about 120 miles, as well as a hybrid minivan dubbed "Freedom." GM has also begun marketing for commercial use an electric van, the G van, powered by lead acid batteries. Chrysler is developing an electric van (the TEVan) based on its popular minivan and powered by nickel-iron batteries. Scheduled for production in 1993, the van has a top speed of about 65 mph and a range of over 120 miles. Ford has developed a new compact drivetrain for electric vehicles that promises lighter weight and increased range. Like GM and Chrysler, Ford is developing an electric van that is likely to be powered by sodium-sulfur batteries.

The emission of greenhouse gases from an electric vehicle depends on the emissions of the power plant that produces the electricity to charge it. If electric vehicles are charged by electricity from the expected mix of coal, oil, gas, nuclear, and hydro plants in the year 2000, greenhouse gas emissions per mile driven would fall by about 25 percent. Charging them with electricity made from coal, in contrast, could increase greenhouse gas emissions by 10 to 30 percent.[56] In the longer term, emissions could be reduced to zero by recharging the batteries using either renewable electricity sources or nuclear power plants.

Currently, hydrogen can be stored in a vehicle using either metal-hydride storage tanks or specially insulated tanks for liquid hydrogen. Prototype hydrogen vehicles are being developed in Japan and Germany. Mercedes-Benz started testing hydrogen-powered vehicles as early as 1974 and has tested sedans, station wagons, vans, and small buses. The most promising means of storing hydrogen is in hydride tanks, where the hydrogen is absorbed by special metal powders (such as titanium-iron and magnesium-nickel) that have a strong attraction for hydrogen. The hydrogen is liberated from these compounds when the tank is heated.

Today's hydride tanks typically weigh about 800 pounds and store only the equivalent of four gallons of gasoline. As a result, present vehicles have driving ranges of only 75 miles. The development of commercial fuel cells, still at least a decade away, would greatly extend the driving range of hydrogen powered cars, trucks, and buses. Fuel cells chemically convert hydrogen and oxygen into water and electricity and would effectively make the hydrogen vehicle a highly efficient electric vehicle.

The pollution-control benefits of this approach are clear. Today's hydrogen powered vehicles emit only water vapor (also emitted by gasoline powered vehicles) and trace amounts of nitrogen oxides, the latter easily controlled with existing technology.

While research and development on new vehicular energy sources goes on, carbon dioxide and pollution emissions in large metropolitan areas can be mitigated through the wider use of natural gas (methane) or methanol to power trucks, buses, and auto fleets. Light-duty vehicles powered by compressed natural gas emit about 15 percent less carbon dioxide per vehicle mile than comparable gasoline-powered vehicles and far less carbon monoxide and volatile organic compounds.[57] In light-duty vehicles, methanol derived from natural gas may offer air pollution benefits but produces about as much carbon dioxide per mile driven as gasoline.

So-called "reformulated gasoline" can also be used as an interim measure to reduce vehicular air pollution. ARCO has already introduced a non-leaded reformulated gasoline, EC-1, to reduce emissions from older, lead-burning vehicles. The company's tests show that if all current users of leaded regular gasoline in southern California switched to EC-1, the air pollution impact would be equivalent to permanently removing 20 percent of the highest-polluting vehicles from the road.[58] According to EPA, reformulated gasoline has the potential to reduce air pollution emissions by 15 to 30 percent.[59] Here again, though, the switch would have little or no impact on carbon dioxide emissions.

4. Reducing Other Greenhouse Gas Emissions

Along with carbon dioxide, the tropospheric ozone (smog), carbon monoxide, and chlorofluorocarbons that motor vehicles discharge or help form, contribute to global warming. As noted, the growth in the number and use of vehicles has largely canceled out the pollution-reduction gains achieved so far, even though almost half of all new cars currently produced around the world are equipped with state-of-the-art emissions controls. But adopting the most technologically advanced controls for carbon monoxide, hydrocarbon, and nitrogen oxides on *all* vehicles throughout the world could at least temporarily restrain the growth in global emissions of these pollutants.

Various steps can be taken to reduce air pollution emissions from motor vehicles. These include incentives to remove older, polluting vehicles from the road; tightening new-vehicle emission standards for nitrogen oxides, volatile organic compounds, and carbon monoxide; developing and using cleaner fuels with lower volatility and fewer toxic components; enhancing inspection and maintenance (I&M) programs, including inspections of anti-tampering emission-control equipment; and extending the useful life for pollution-control equipment to ten years or 100,000 miles rather than the current five years or 50,000 miles. The potential

overall impacts of tighter standards, enhanced inspection and maintenance, and extended useful life are especially significant because they help ensure that the benefits of clean-air technology will persist for the vehicle's full life.

The production of CFCs, the most potent greenhouse gases, will be drastically cut by the revised Montreal Protocol, adopted in June 1990. Thanks to the new international agreement, CFC production will cease by the year 2000. This landmark decision—a major first step toward controlling greenhouse gas emissions—provides a precedent for future negotiations and cooperation.

Future CFC releases could be greatly reduced by improving air conditioner seals and, especially, by changing work practices in repair shops. Eliminating the use of CFCs in automotive air conditioners or, in the short term, prohibiting unnecessary venting to the air, would protect the stratosphere from ozone depletion and reduce greenhouse warming. What is needed over the long term is cradle-to-grave controls designed to eliminate CFC emissions from vehicles. A comprehensive CFC-control strategy would require that hoses, seals, and fittings on air conditioners last for the vehicle's full life without leaking; limit repair of air conditioners to qualified, licensed facilities that use equipment designed to prevent leakage or venting of CFCs; and ban the sale of do-it-yourself kits to recharge auto air conditioners. A number of auto-makers, including General Motors, Ford, Toyota, and Honda have indicated their plans to install in each of their dealerships equipment that will capture the CFCs from motor vehicle air conditioners.

* * *

The development of petroleum-powered motor vehicles has truly revolutionized society over the past century. The benefits of increased personal mobility and access to goods and services previously beyond the grasp of individuals cannot be denied. And, yet, the relentless growth in motor vehicle use has a dark downside that Americans have been slow to acknowledge, including a growing dependency on imported oil and a broad array of adverse public health and environmental impacts.

The environmental damages caused by motor vehicle emissions are no longer debatable, and on a global basis they are increasing. The cars, trucks, and buses that make life better in so many ways emit more than 800 million tons of carbon per year. From their tailpipes come virtually all of the carbon monoxide in the air of our cities. Less directly, they cause much of the ozone and smog. And motor vehicles play a significant role in stratospheric ozone depletion. All of these pollutants contribute directly or indirectly to global warming.

Over the last forty years, the global vehicle fleet has grown from under 50 million to more than 500 million, and there is every indication that this growth will continue. Over the next twenty years, the global fleet could double to one billion. Unless transportation technology and planning are fundamentally transformed, emissions of greenhouse and other polluting gases from these vehicles will continue to increase, many relatively clean environments will deteriorate, and the few areas that have made progress will see some of their gains eroded.

The worldwide challenges that these problems pose for motor vehicle manufacturers and policy-makers are unprecedented. Nothing less than a revolution in technology and thinking at least as profound as the initial mechanization of transportation is needed. Manufacturers will come under increasing pressures to produce petroleum-powered vehicles that are ever cleaner, safer, more reliable, and more fuel efficient. At the same time, they will need to develop new kinds of vehicles that will emit no pollution whatever. The amount of capital needed to accomplish these goals will be large and, making matters even more difficult, the pressures for these changes will arise not so much from traditional market forces but from public policies adopted in response to climate and other threats.

Fortunately, the global motor vehicle industry is sufficiently concentrated that swift technological change will be possible once the need becomes more widely recognized. Indeed, if only fourteen manufacturers and their subsidiaries modified their vehicle designs, emissions from one of the largest sources of atmospheric pollution could be dramatically reduced. Clearly, the burden is on a handful of countries to design vehicles with the environmental future, and not just styling and performance, in mind.

James J. MacKenzie is a physicist and senior associate in World Resources Institute's Program on Climate, Energy, and Pollution. He has published widely on air pollution and energy issues.
Michael P. Walsh is an international consultant on transportation and environmental issues. He is former director of the U.S. EPA motor vehicle pollution control program.

Notes

1. *World Resources*, 1990–1991, Chapter 2, "Climate Change: A Global Concern," Oxford University Press, New York, 1990.

2. John Gribbin, "The Hole in the Sky, Man's Threat to the Ozone Layer," Bantam Books, New York, 1988.

3. Press Release, May 25, 1990, Intergovernmental Panel on Climate Change, Working Group 1, Scientific Assessment of Climate Change.

4. *World Resources*, 1990–1991, Chapter 2, "Climate Change: A Global Concern," Oxford University Press, New York, 1990.

5. Lower value from "Regional Greenhouse Climate Effects," J. Hansen et al., Proceedings of the Second North American Conference on Preparing for Climate Change, December 6–8, 1988. Climate Institute, Washington, D.C., p. 79. Larger value from "The Potential Effects of Global Climate Change on the United States," U.S. EPA, EPA-230-05-89-050, December 1989, p. 13.

6. "An Evaluation of the Relationship Between the Production and Use of Energy and Atmospheric Methane Emissions," U.S. Department of Energy, DOE/NBB-0088P, April 1990, p. 1.4.

7. "An Emissions Inventory for SO_2, NO_x, and VOC's in North-Western Europe," Lubkert, de Tilly, Organization for Economic Cooperation and Development, 1987.

8. U.S. Environmental Protection Agency, "The Potential Effects of Global Climate Change on the United States," December 1989, EPA-230-05-89-050, p. 15.

9. Press Release, May 25, 1990, Intergovernmental Panel on Climate Change, Working Group 1, Scientific Assessment of Climate Change. For discussions of the various possible impacts see the pertinent chapters of "World Resources, 1990–91," World Resources Institute, Oxford University Press, New York, 1990.

10. Executive Summary, "Policy Options for Stabilizing Global Climate," Environmental Protection Agency, Draft to Congress, February 1989, p. 26.

11. "Policymakers Summary of the Scientific Assessment of Climate Change, Report to IPCC from Working Group 1," May 2, 1990 Draft.

12. The remaining impacts are discussed in various chapters in *The Challenge of Global Warming*, edited by Dean E. Abrahamson, Island Press, Washington, D.C., 1989.

13. Press Release from IPCC Working Group 1, Scientific Assessment of Climate Change, May 25, 1990.

14. DeLuchi, M.A. et. al., "Transportation Fuels and the Greenhouse Effect," *Transportation Research Record*, Vol. 1175, 1988.

15. A. Volz & D. Kley, "Evaluation of the Montsouris Series of Ozone Measurements Made in the Nineteenth Century," *Nature* 332 (1988) 240–43.

16. "Sources, Sinks, Trends, and Opportunities," by Peter Ciborowski, in *The Challenge of Global Warming*, edited by Dean E. Abrahamson, Island Press, Washington, D.C., 1989, p. 217.

17. Sanford Sillman, Jennifer A. Logan, and Steven C. Wofsy, "Sensitivity of Ozone to Nitrogen Oxides and Hydrocarbons in Regional Ozone Episodes," *Journal of Geophysical Research*, Vol. 95: 1837–1851, Feb. 20, 1990.

18. "Health Effects of Ambient Air Pollution," American Lung Association, New York, N.Y., July 1989.

19. "Air Pollution's Toll on Forests and Crops," edited by James J. MacKenzie and Mohamed T. El-Ashry, Yale University Press, New Haven, 1989.

20. "National Air Quality and Emissions Trends Report, 1988" US EPA, EPA-450/4-90-002, March 1990, p. 15.

21. "Health Effects of Ambient Air Pollution," American Lung Association, 1989, p. 10.

22. "National Air Quality and Emissions Trends Report, 1988" US EPA, EPA-450/4-90-002, March 1990, pp. 6 and 15.

23. Khalil, M.A.K. & Rasmussen, R.A., "Carbon Monoxide in the Earth's Atmosphere: Indications of a Global Increase," 332 *Nature* 245 (March, 1988).

24. "World Resources 1988–89," Basic Books, Inc., New York, 1988, p. 168.

25. "National Air Quality and Emissions Trends Report, 1988" US EPA, EPA-450/4-90-002, March 1990, p. 56.

26. "Air Quality Criteria for Ozone and Other Photochemical Oxidants," Vol II, US EPA, EPA/600/8-84/020bF, August 1986, p. 3–15 ff.

27. "The Hole in the Sky, Man's Threat to the Ozone Layer," John Gribbin, Bantam Books, New York, 1988.

28. "Technical Progress on Protecting the Ozone Layer," Refrigeration, Air Conditioning and Heat Pumps Technical Options Report, UNEP Technology Review Panel, July 30, 1989.

29. "How Industry is Reducing Dependence on Ozone-Depleting Chemicals," A Status Report Prepared by the Stratospheric Ozone Protection Program, US EPA, June 1988, p. 10.

30. Update to "How Industry is Reducing Dependence on Ozone-Depleting Chemicals," A Status Report Prepared by the Stratospheric Ozone Protection Program, provided by US EPA, draft, 1990.

31. "World Motor Vehicle Data, 1990 Edition," Motor Vehicle Manufacturers Association of the United States, Inc., p. 35.

32. "Facts and Figures '89," Motor Vehicle Manufacturers Association, p. 28.

33. "World Motor Vehicle Data, 1990 Edition," Motor Vehicle Manufacturers Association of the United States, Inc., pp., 36–38.

34. In this report, carbon dioxide emissions are calculated from OECD data contained in the following reports: "Energy Balances of OECD Countries, 1970/1985," "Energy Balances of OECD Countries, 1986/1987," and "World Energy Statistics and Balances, 1971–1987." For each country, the annual

values of oil consumed in road transport were used to calculate direct carbon dioxide emissions from motor vehicles. Indirect emissions, from the production, processing, and transport of motor vehicle fuels, are not included here.

35. "Monthly Energy Review," January 1990, US Department of Energy, published April 1990. DOE/EIA-0035(90/01), p. 15.

36. "Changing Driving Patterns and Their Effect on Fuel Economy," Fred Westbrook and Phil Patterson, presented May 2, 1989 at the 1989 SAE Government/Industry Meeting, Washington, D.C.

37. "Transportation Energy to the Year 2020," by D.L. Greene, D. Sperling, and B. McNutt, in *A Look Ahead, Year 2020*, Transportation Research Board, National Research Council, Washington, D.C., 1988, p. 217.

38. "Downward Trend in Passenger Car Fuel Economy—A View of Recent Data," J. Dillard Murrell and Robert M. Heavenrich, EPA/AA/CTAB/90-01, January 1990.

39. "Facts and Figures, '89," MVMA, pp. 16 and 19.

40. "Facts and Figures, '89," MVMA, p. 75.

41. "Summary of Travel Trends," 1983–1984 Nationwide Personal Transportation Study, U.S. Department of Transportation, Nov. 1985, p. 14.

42. *Ibid.*

43. "Our Nation's Highways, Selected Facts and Figures," U.S. Department of Transportation, Office of Highway Information Management, 1990, p. 3.

44. *Automotive News, 1990 Market Data Book,* May 30, 1990, p. 189.

45. *Ibid.*

46. Committee on Motor Vehicle Emissions for the Australian Transport Advisory Council, "Report on the Development of a Long-term National Motor Vehicle Emissions Strategy," 1981.

Environmental Protection Service, "Air Pollution Emissions and Controls, Heavy Duty Vehicles," Ottawa, Ontario, Canada, September 1986.

Gillingham, S.G., Tabulated Statistical Data, Department of Transport, London, August, 1988.

Hui-Chuan Hsiao, Personal Communication, June 1988.

Jakeman, A.J., "Urban Motor Vehicle Travel to the Year 2010, June 1987.

Madden, Richard L., "Traffic Perils Economic Boom of Suburbs Around New York." *New York Times,* Monday, July 4, 1988.

Mujawar, Z.A., "Statistics on Vehicle Production and Registration," The Automotive Research Association of India, July, 1988. Bombay: The Automotive Components Manufacturers Association, (ACMA), Bombay and Association of Indian Automobile Manufacturers (AIAM), Bombay.

Myers, Stephen. "Transport in the LDCs: A Major Area of Growth in World Oil Demand." Berkeley, CA, March, 1988.

Naturvardsverket Rapport 3261. *Utslapp av luftfororeningar fran framtida personbilar.*

OCDE, OECD. *Long Term Outlook for the World Automobile Industry*, Paris, 1983.

Registry of Vehicles, *Registry of Vehicles Annual Report, 1986,* Singapore.

Saudi Arabian Standards Organization. *A Guide to Saudi Motor Vehicle Standards,* January, 1985.

_____, *List of Saudi Standards,* 1987/1407.

Sverker Sjostrom, tekn dr. *The Motor Vehicle, Aircraft and the Environment.* Sweden, 1988.

Strategic Analysis Europe. *Overview of the West European Motor Vehicle Market,* July, 1988.

The Australian Bureau of Statistics, "Motor Vehicle Registrations, Australia," April, 1988.

The New Zealand Motor Trade Federation. *Motor Industry Year Book,* Wellington, New Zealand, 1987.

Transport Canada, *1988 Fuel Consumption Guide, Guide De Consommation De Carburant 1988,* Canada: Ministre des Approvisionnements et Services Canada, 1987.

R. Rothan, Data on Vehicle Populations and Fuel Consumption, Switzerland, Personal Communication, June 21, 1988.

Erik Iversen, Personal Communication, July 1988.

Martin Kroon, Mobile Source Control Strategies in the Netherlands, Atmospheric Ozone Research & Its Policy Implications, Third US-Dutch International Symposium, May 9–13, 1988.

Transport Canada, Nitrogen Oxides (NO$_x$): Information Package For The Special Committee On Acid Rain, House of Commons, May 12, 1988.

DG III, Commission of the European Communities, Draft Paper on Composition of EC-Petrol Car Market and Parc, and on Kilometrage by Classes of Engine Capacity, January 1985.

S. Gospage, DGIII, Commission of the European Communities, Diesel Cars in the European Community, April 26, 1985.

S. Gospage, DG III, Commission of the European Communities, The EC Parc of Vehicles Below 3.5 Tonnes, 1984-2000, April 26, 1985.

S. Gospage, DG III, Commission of the European Communities, Environmental Impact of New EEC Exhaust Emission Standards for NO$_x$ Compared to those In Force in the USA, 1985.

Raisa Valli, Personal Communication, Finland Ministry of the Environment, July 7, 1988.

May Grethe Svenningsen (B.A.), Age Pran, Personal Communication, Norway State Pollution Control Authority, July 11, 1988.

Dr. Karl-Johann Hartig, Personal Communication, Bundesministerium Fur Offentliche Wirtschaft und Verkehr, Buro des Bundesministers, July 12, 1988.

Prof. Dr. H.P. Lenz, "Schadstoffemissionen von Kraftfahrzeugen in Osterreich," Institut Fur Verbrennungskraftmaschinen und Kraftfahrzeugbau, Technische Universitat Wien, November 1985.

Deutsche Shell Aktiengesellschaft, Frauen bestimmen die weitere Motorisierung, Shell-Prognose des PKW-Bestandes bis zum Jahr 2000, Hamburg, September 1987.

ADAC, Mobilitat Untersuchungen und Antworten des ADAC zu den Fragen, June 1987.

Swiss Federal Institute of Technology Zurich, Test Procedures and Standards For Heavy Duty Engine Emissions (Total Weight > 3500 Kg), ETHZ-Proposal for a Second Phase, June 20, 1987.

Larsolov Olsson, Swedish Environmental Protection Board, Data on Swedish Vehicle Fleet for Mobile 3, May 23, 1986.

Masatoshi Matsunami, Director Engineering and Planning Division, Land Transport

Engineering Department, Ministry of Transport, Japan, Personal Communication, June 13, 1988.

47. "Population Studies No. 106, World Population Prospects 1988" Department of International Economic and Social Affairs, United Nations, New York, 1989.

48. "Facts and Figures, '89" Motor Vehicle Manufacturers Association of the United States, Inc. p. 52.

49. "Changing Driving Patterns and their Effect on Fuel Economy," Fred Westbrook and Phil Patterson, presented May 2, 1989 at the 1989 SAE Government/Industry Meeting, Washington, D.C.

50. "Facts and Figures, '90" Motor Vehicle Manufacturers Association of the United States, 1990, p. 51.

51. "Policy Options for Stabilizing Global Climate," Draft Report to Congress, Executive Summary, Feb. 1989, p. 15.

52. Deborah L. Bleviss, *The New Oil Crisis and Fuel Economy Technologies*, Quorum Books, Westport, Connecticut, 1988.

53. "World Resources, 1990–91," Oxford University Press, New York, 1990, pp. 148–152.

54. "Advanced Vehicle/Highway Systems and Urban Traffic Problems," Staff Paper, Science, Education, and Transportation Program, Office of Technology Assessment, U.S. Congress, September 1989.

55. "Application of Ultracapacitors in Electric Vehicle Propulsion Systems," A.F. Burke, J.E. Hardin, (both of Idaho National Engineering Laboratory), and E.J. Dowgiallo (DOE), paper presented at 34th International Power Sources Symposium, June 25–28, 1990.

56. "Replacing Gasoline, Alternative Fuels for Light-Duty Vehicles," Office of Technology Assessment, U.S. Congress, September, 1990, p. 20.

57. *New Transportation Fuels, A Strategic Approach to Technological Change*, Daniel Sperling, U. of California Press, Berkeley, CA, 1988, p. 326.

58. "Alternative Motor Vehicle Fuels to Improve Air Quality, Options and Implications for California," California Council for Environmental and Economic Balance, San Francisco, CA, 1990, p. 66.

59. *Ibid.*

World Resources Institute

1709 New York Avenue, N.W.
Washington, D.C. 20006, U.S.A.

The World Resources Institute (WRI) is a policy research center created in late 1982 to help governments, international organizations, and private business address a fundamental question: How can societies meet basic human needs and nurture economic growth without undermining the natural resources and environmental integrity on which life, economic vitality, and international security depend?

Two dominant concerns influence WRI's choice of projects and other activities:

The destructive effects of poor resource management on economic development and the alleviation of poverty in developing countries; and

The new generation of globally important environmental and resource problems that threaten the economic and environmental interests of the United States and other industrial countries and that have not been addressed with authority in their laws.

The Institute's current areas of policy research include tropical forests, biological diversity, sustainable agriculture, energy, climate change, atmospheric pollution, economic incentives for sustainable development, and resource and environmental information.

WRI's research is aimed at providing accurate information about global resources and population, identifying emerging issues, and developing politically and economically workable proposals.

In developing countries, WRI provides field services and technical program support for governments and non-governmental organizations trying to manage natural resources sustainably.

WRI's work is carried out by an interdisciplinary staff of scientists and experts augmented by a network of formal advisors, collaborators, and cooperating institutions in 50 countries.

WRI is funded by private foundations, United Nations and governmental agencies, corporations, and concerned individuals.